A SWORD TO THE HEART

From the moment she saw him, Natalia Grey-
stroke knew that Lord Ranulf Colwall was the
one man she could love. And when he asked to
marry her, she thought he felt the same way. But
on her wedding night, Natalia overheard her
husband say that he would never permit himself
to love any woman—all he desired from marriage
was an heir to his vast estate.

Natalia was crushed. She knew she could never
truly become Lord Colwall's wife. Desperate and
afraid, she fled her new home—still hoping she
had kindled some spark of affection that would
bring him to her side.

BARBARA CARTLAND

Books by BARBARA CARTLAND

Romantic Novels

The Fire of Love
The Unpredictable Bride
Love Holds the Cards
A Virgin in Paris
Love to the Rescue
Love Is Contraband
The Enchanting Evil
The Unknown Heart
The Secret Fear
The Reluctant Bride
The Pretty Horse-Breakers
The Audacious Adventuress
Lost Enchantment
Halo for the Devil
The Irresistible Buck

The Complacent Wife
The Odious Duke
The Daring Deception
No Darkness for Love
The Little Adventure
Lessons in Love
Journey to Paradise
The Bored Bridegroom
The Penniless Peer
The Dangerous Dandy
The Ruthless Rake
The Wicked Marquis
The Castle of Fear
The Glittering Lights
A Sword to the Heart

Autobiographical and Biographical

The Isthmus Years 1919–1939
The Years of Opportunity
   1939–1945
I Search for Rainbows 1945–1966
We Danced All Night 1919–1929

Ronald Cartland
   (with a Foreword
   by Sir Winston Churchill)
Polly, My Wonderful Mother

Historical

Bewitching Women
The Outrageous Queen
   (The Story of
   Queen Christina of Sweden)
The Scandalous Life of King Carol
The Private Life of King Charles II

The Private Life of Elizabeth,
   Empress of Austria
Josephine, Empress of France
Diane de Poitiers
Metternich—
   the Passionate Diplomat

Sociology

You in the Home
The Fascinating Forties
Marriage for Moderns
Be Vivid, Be Vital
Love, Life and Sex
Look Lovely, Be Lovely
Vitamins for Vitality
Husbands and Wives

Etiquette
The Many Facets of Love
Sex and the Teenager
The Book of Charm
Living Together
Woman—The Enigma
The Youth Secret
The Magic of Honey

Barbara Cartland's Health Food Cookery Book
Barbara Cartland's Book of Beauty and Health
Men Are Wonderful

A Sword
to the Heart

Barbara Cartland

BANTAM BOOKS
TORONTO · NEW YORK · LONDON

A SWORD TO THE HEART
A Bantam Book / published December 1974

PRINTING HISTORY

Published simultaneously in the United States and Canada

Bantam Books are published by Bantam Books, Inc. Its trade-
mark, consisting of the words "Bantam Books" and the por-
trayal of a bantam, is registered in the United States Patent
Office and in other countries. Marca Registrada. Bantam
Books, Inc., 666 Fifth Avenue, New York, New York 10019.

PRINTED IN THE UNITED STATES OF AMERICA

Author's Note

The Labourers' revolt in 1830 was extremely serious. Several Counties in the South of England were in a state bordering on insurrection. The Government was in a panic. The rebellion failed completely although there was some improvement in the farm workers' wages. Six men were hanged, four hundred imprisoned and four hundred and fifty-seven transported. Three boats carried the convicts to Van Dieman's Land and New South Wales. The list of prisoners shows they came from thirteen different Counties, but there was no-one from Herefordshire.

There are innumerable legends about the famous "Captain Swing," whose threatening letters spread terror among the landowners of England. It has never been satisfactorily established if he was or was not hanged with several other leaders of the riots.

A Sword
to the Heart

Chapter One

1830

"Lord Colwall to see you, Sir James."

A middle-aged man sitting by the fire reading a newspaper rose with an exclamation of surprise.

Advancing towards him across the room was a young man, elegantly attired with a meticulously tied high cravat and a jewelled fob glittering below his cut-away coat.

He was in fact extremely handsome with fine-cut features and dark hair above a square forehead, but there was an expression on his face which at first acquaintance seemed almost repellent.

It was hard to believe that a man so young in years should look so cynical and at the same time so proudly aloof that a stranger might instinctively shrink from contact with him.

But Sir James Parke was an old friend, and the way in which he held out his hand and the smile on his lips showed that he was sincerely pleased by the intrusion.

"Ranulf!" he cried. "Why did you not let me know you were coming? But none the less it is a great pleasure to see you."

Lord Colwall did not smile in response. Instead, he joined Sir James in front of the log-blazing fire and replied in a cold, almost expressionless, voice:

"I made up my mind to visit you only yesterday evening."

Sir James looked at the young man's face a little apprehensively.

"Is there anything wrong at the Castle?"

"No, nothing."

Sir James waited as if for more information, and when it was not forthcoming, he said genially:

"Do sit down, Ranulf. What will you have to drink? A glass of Port? Or would you prefer Madeira at this hour of the morning?"

He put out his hand towards the bell-pull as he spoke.

"Thank you, but I have not long breakfasted," Lord Colwall said before he could ring the bell.

"I have just been reading *The Times,*" Sir James said, "about the threatening letters written to landlords in the Southern Counties and signed 'Swing.' It seems extraordinary that no-one knows who this man is."

The two gentlemen seated themselves opposite each other at the fireside.

"When they do discover his identity," Lord Colwall replied, "he will surely be hanged, or at least transported."

"There are all sorts of rumours about him," Sir James said, "that he is a disgruntled Peer or a criminal who has escaped the gallows, or a lawyer who has been barred from practising."

Lord Colwall did not reply and Sir James went on:

"Whoever he may be—and I imagine he is an educated man from the manner in which he writes—he is undoubtedly responsible for the riots around Canterbury. Farm-workers could never organise such a rebellion by themselves. There must be someone behind them."

"That is obvious," Lord Colwall said in a hard voice, "and they have been innoculated with this man's poison. Did you hear what a labourer said to the High Sheriff of Kent?"

"No, tell me," Sir James said.

"Apparently the High Sheriff attended one of the College meetings to remonstrate with the rioters. They listened to his homily with attention. But before they dispersed a man said:

" 'This year we will destroy the corn-stacks and the threshing machines, next year we will have a turn with the parsons, and the third we will make war upon the Statesmen.' "

"Good God!" Sir James ejaculated. "That will be Civil War!"

"It will be now if the Government does not use a firmer hand than they are doing at the moment," Lord Colwall remarked.

"Reading some of the letters in *The Times*," Sir James said, "I cannot help feeling that the labourers have a case."

"A case?" Lord Colwall ejaculated sharply. "They have nothing of the sort! They are paid for their work, and to burn ricks and break up farm machinery is sheer anarchy, as you well know."

There was now almost a note of violence in the cold voice and, because Sir James Parke was a man who enjoyed peace and disliked argument, he said in a conciliatory tone:

"Let us talk of something more pleasant. What brings you on this most welcome visit?"

Lord Colwall hesitated as if he was considering his words, then he replied slowly:

"I came to ask you, Sir James, if you would be best man at my wedding."

For a moment Sir James Parke stared incredulously, then he exclaimed:

"At your wedding? My dear boy I can assure you that nothing would give me greater pleasure! I had no idea—no-one told me that you were even contemplating matrimony. Have I missed the announcement of your engagement?"

"There has been no announcement," Lord Colwall replied.

"And who is the bride? Do I know her?"

"No, you do not know her."

As Lord Colwall spoke he rose to his feet and

walked across the room to the window to stand staring out at the elaborate garden, to which his host devoted a great deal of his time and thought.

Sir James looked at his broad shoulders in perplexity.

"What is all this about, Ranulf?" he said at length. "As you well know, nothing would delight me more than to see you married."

"I am aware of that," Lord Colwall said, turning from the window. "It is because you were a friend of my father, Sir James, and because until I was twenty-five you acted as my Trustee, that you are the first person to learn of my intended nuptials."

"I am indeed honoured by your confidence," Sir James said, "but why is it a secret?"

"It is no secret," Lord Colwall answered. "It is in fact something I have planned for a long time."

"You have planned?"

Lord Colwall came back from the window to the fireplace.

"When Claris left me," he said slowly, as if he forced the words between his lips, "I swore that I would never marry again."

"You were distraught at the time," Sir James said quietly. "You had been badly treated, Ranulf, as we know, and at the same time you were very young. You had not even reached your twenty-first year, and under such circumstances one says things that one does not mean."

"I meant every word of it!" Lord Colwall contradicted, "but three years ago, when I was twenty-five and came into full possession of my properties, I realised that, whatever my personal feelings in the matter, I must for the sake of the family beget an heir."

Sir James looked at him quickly before he said:

"You are right, of course. There have been Colwalls at the Castle since the twelfth century."

"Exactly!" Lord Colwall agreed. "And that is why the inheritance must continue in the direct line. I intend, Sir James, when I die to hand the Castle over to my son!"

"That of course is what we would all wish to happen!" Sir James agreed. "And I would like above all else, Ranulf, to see you happy."

"I am entirely content as I am," Lord Colwall said coldly, "but since I cannot have a legitimate son without a wife, I have therefore chosen one!"

"Who is she?" Sir James asked. "One of our local belles? Or have you found some 'Incomparable' in London who will bring grace and beauty to our rather dull countryside?"

"I told you," Lord Colwall went on, as if he had not listened to what Sir James was saying, "that I have planned my marriage with care. That is precisely the truth."

There was a note in his voice which brought a little frown between Sir James's eyes.

"What are you trying to tell me, Ranulf?"

"I am attempting to explain what I have done," Lord Colwall replied, "not because I need your approval, but simply because I feel that you, who have always been so closely concerned with my affairs, should know the truth."

"And what is the truth?" Sir James enquired.

"When I decided to get married again," Lord Colwall replied, "I knew that the one thing I could not face was to marry another wife who might behave like Claris. I have learnt, Sir James, by bitter experience that what is loosely called love can be a weapon of self-destruction."

"Now, Ranulf, you are still bitter, still resentful of what happened eight years ago," Sir James interposed. "Surely you can understand now that the emotions through which you passed were unusual, to say the least of it, in fact a disaster which might happen to perhaps one man in a million."

"I can only hope your figures are right!" Lord Colwall said with a cynical twist of his lips.

"Now that you are older and wiser," Sir James went on, "you can forget the past. You have your life in front of you. You have a position that men envy. You have great possessions, a heritage which is steeped in the history of England, and a name which is respected throughout the land."

"Exactly!" Lord Colwall ejaculated, "and that is why, since my name is respected, and since I was fool enough to put at risk both the honour and the pride of my family, I shall not make the same mistake again."

"You could not have known at your age what Claris was like," Sir James said. "You were infatuated with her beauty, and who shall blame you? No-one could have anticipated what occurred."

"You yourself warned me that I was taking a risk in marrying her," Lord Colwall said harshly, "but I would not listen."

"You were in love," Sir James said quietly, "and all must be forgiven if a man loses his head in such circumstances."

"I was besotted, infatuated and bewitched until I behaved like a damned idiot!" Lord Colwall said roughly. "It will never happen again."

"We all make mistakes in our lives," Sir James said soothingly. "We all make jackasses of ourselves at some time or another. But what I had always hoped, Ranulf, is that as the years passed you would forget; your bitterness would pass and one day you would find a woman you could love and who would love you."

"I remember telling you when I learned the truth about Claris, that I would never love anyone again," Lord Colwall answered. "It was not the statement of an hysterical boy, Sir James. It was in the nature of a vow, a vow to which I shall adhere to my dying day."

"And yet you are to be married?"

"I am to be married for the reason I have given you," Lord Colwall answered. "I chose my wife three years ago when she was fifteen. She has now passed her eighteenth birthday and she is at this moment on her way from Cumberland, where she lives, to the Castle. She will arrive next Wednesday and the marriage has been planned for the following day at which I hope you will support me."

"What do you mean—you chose her when she was fifteen?" Sir James enquired.

"Exactly what I have said," Lord Colwall answered. "I made a list of my relations and close connections who had girls of about the right age. I visited them."

There was a faint note of amusement in his voice as he said:

"In Lincolnshire I found that a third cousin once removed had a daughter of the right age, but her mother was a hopeless drunkard!"

Sir James said nothing and Lord Colwell continued:

"Sixty miles further north another relative produced a girl with a squint and the suspicion of a harelip! Hardly encouraging characteristics!"

There was still no response from Sir James.

"Then at Pooley Bridge in Cumberland," His Lordship continued, "I found my father's second cousin, Lady Margaret Graystoke, had a daughter aged fifteen."

Lord Colwall glanced at Sir James, who was sitting listening intently, his eyes on his face.

"Lady Margaret's antecedents are impeccable," he continued, "and Graystoke comes from an old and respected Cumberland family. His brother is the fifth Baronet. They have little money, but their breeding is faultless!"

"Are you telling me," Sir James asked with an astonished note in his voice, "that you chose this girl whom you are to marry as if you were buying a foal?"

"Why not?" Lord Colwall answered. "After all, the reason I require her as a wife is simply that she should produce children."

"Have you told the girl this?"

"I have not seen her since I visited her father's Vicarage three years ago."

"You have not—seen her?"

Sir James rose to his feet.

"My dear Ranulf, this is monstrous! This is the most crazy, insane action I have ever heard! You cannot do such a thing!"

Lord Colwall looked at him in surprise.

"What is wrong with it?" he enquired. "If I had met a girl in London, spoken to her perhaps two or three times under the eyes of her mother, and then asked if

I might pay her my addresses, you would not have
been in the least surprised. But I would know as much
or as little about her as I know about Natalia."

"A girl you saw once as a child?" Sir James insisted.
"What was she like?"

"She was pleasant-looking," he replied, "with no ap-
parent physical imperfections. A little short perhaps,
but doubtless she has grown. As I have already said,
she comes of good stock, and I cannot imagine that
the daughter of a poverty-stricken Vicar would not feel
honoured to be the Chatelaine of Colwall Castle."

"In other words, you take for granted that she is
selling herself for your title and your position, and you
are buying her to act as a breeding machine!" Sir James
said.

For the first time Lord Colwall gave a faint smile.

"You are very dramatic, Sir James, but I assure you
that a *mariage de convenance* is far more likely to be
successful than one which rests upon throbbing hearts,
passionate declarations, and that deceptive emotion
called love."

"Supposing when you meet the girl again you dislike
one another?" Sir James asked. "What then?"

"She will still have her position as my wife," Lord
Colwall explained patiently. "and I shall hope to have
not only an heir, but several children."

"It is the most unnatural thing I have ever heard,"
Sir James said crossly. "Now listen to me, Ranulf, for
one moment."

"I am listening," Lord Colwall replied.

"You are an extremely attractive young man. There
is not a young woman in the whole length and breadth
of Herefordshire who would not fall into your arms if
you gave her the slightest encouragement. The girls
have told me how you seem to rebuff every overture
they have made in your direction. That is not to say
they would not go on making them!"

"I am well aware of that!" Lord Colwall replied.

"And surely," Sir James went on, "there have been
women in London whose company you have enjoyed."

There was a cynical twist to Lord Colwall's lips as he replied:

"Many of them, but they were hardly suitable, either by birth or by education to sit at the top of my table."

"I am not talking about strumpets!" Sir James said sharply. "You have moved in the society of what in my day, when the Regent considered himself a gay Lothario, we used to call 'The Dandy Set.' Surely in that crowd there must have been beautiful women who attracted your attention?"

"Quite a number," Lord Colwall replied frankly, "but they had the great advantage, from my point of view, of already having a husband, even if he was a complaisant one. And while they certainly pleased my eye and, shall we say, excited my interest, I did not find any difficulty in parting from them once they bored me."

"Good God, Ranulf! You must have a heart somewhere in that handsome body of yours?"

"A heart?" Lord Colwall inquired mockingly. "I assure you, my dear Sir James, I tore that vacillating vessel from my breast and replaced it with a stone! I have no heart! No tenderness! No love! And, I hope, no vulnerability left in what you call 'my handsome body.'

"I am a man with the normal passions of a man, but I am completely armoured against the wiles and the deceits of women."

"And you really think you can live the rest of your life in such a state?" Sir James asked.

"I am sure of it," Lord Colwall answered confidently, "and let me tell you that I am absolutely content with myself as I am. People speak of me as a hard man—I am well aware of that! I am hard! I am ruthless! And I intend to stay that way. I do not wish to be beguiled and enticed up the aisle by any designing female, who covets my name."

"It would be easy for a woman to love you for yourself," Sir James said quietly.

"That is where you are wrong!" Lord Colwall contradicted. "No woman will ever love me again because I do not intend that she should do so. I willl take her body if it amuses me, but I am not interested in her mind, in her feelings and certainly not in her affections!"

There was a sneer on his lips as he finished.

"Most women, after a few plaintive protestations, are content to take my money or whatever I am prepared to give them and leave me alone."

Sir James gave a deep sigh.

"You were one of the most attractive boys I have ever known. You were a very charming young man. I am not being dramatic, Ranulf, when I say I would have given my right hand to save you from the tragedy which altered your whole character. It should never have happened."

"But it did happen!" Lord Colwall said quietly. "And, as you say, it altered my character and my outlook. There can be no going back. I have therefore made my life my own way! And I can say with complete honesty that it is the way I prefer."

"Perhaps one day . . ." Sir James began tentatively.

"No, no, Sir James," Lord Colwall interrupted. "You are a romantic! This is reality. A man may suffer once from being burnt by a raging fire, but a second time he is too wary to approach it. I have suffered, as you rightly said, but it has made me wise and I shall not make a fool of myself a second time."

"And what about this child that you intend to marry?" Sir James asked.

"Doubtless her parents have explained to her the advantages of such a match," Lord Colwall said loftily, "Incidentally I have paid quite a considerable sum over the years for her education."

"You wanted her educated then?"

"Not for my own benefit," Lord Colwall answered, "but because the mother of my children should be cultured and have a certain amoung of learning. After all, a mother is the first teacher a child knows."

There was silence for a moment and then Sir James said:

"It is a pity you did not know your mother. She was very beautiful and very understanding. I have always been convinced that, had she been alive, you would not have been deceived by Claris."

"She died when I was only a year old, and therefore I cannot remember her," Lord Colwall replied. "On the other hand, I remember my father distinctly. I endured eighteen years of his severity and his unmistakeable indifference."

"Your father was never the same after the death of your mother," Sir James said. "It was his love for her which made him resent that you were alive, and he blamed you because she never recovered from the very difficult time she had when you were born."

"I know that, Lord Colwall remarked, "and it only proves my point, Sir James, that love, obsessive, possessive and demanding is something to be avoided at all costs."

"Perhaps you will be unable to avoid it," Sir James suggested. "It conquers us all at some time in our lives."

"You are living in cloud-cuckoo land!" Lord Colwall sneered. "Now I must ask you if, having heard the truth about my impending wedding, you will still act as my best man?"

"I will do anything you ask of me," Sir James answered simply, "but I am no less worried and perturbed by what you have told me."

"Leave me to do the worrying," Lord Colwall said. "The marriage will take place in the afternoon, and we shall sit down to what will be a Medieval Wedding Feast at about five o'clock."

"Medieval?" Sir James questioned.

"I found some difficulty in discovering amongst the archives any precedent for a marriage feast of the owner or his son taking place in the Castle." Lord Colwall replied. "Of course, the Reception was usually given at the home of the Bride."

"Naturally," Sir James agreed.

"But in 1496," Lord Colwall went on, "Randolph, the elder son of Sir Hereward Colwall, was married at the Castle to a bride who came to him from Northumbria. It seemed, when I found the reference, an interesting coincidence that my wife comes from Cumberland."

"Were they happy?" Sir James enquired.

"As they had eleven children how could they be anything else?" Lord Colwall replied mockingly.

"Then let us hope that for your sake history repeats itself," Sir James said, but he spoke without conviction.

The Dritchka chariot moved along the highway at a quicker pace than had been possible on the previous days of the journey.

"Look, Papa, it has hardly rained here at all!" Natalia exclaimed.

"I believe it has been a dry October in the South," the Reverend Adolphus Graystoke replied in a tired voice.

He had found the long journey somewhat exhausting while it appeared that his daughter was fresher and in gayer spirits than when they had first left their home in Pooley Bridge.

Everything en route was of interest to Natalia; even the rough, muddy roads that they had encountered on the first part of their journey had been no hardship.

This was due to the well-sprung travelling chariot which Lord Colwall had sent for them. When it arrived at the Vicarage, its silver accoutrements and four magnificent horses had evoked the admiration of the whole village.

Even the Vicar had been astonished at the luxury at which they travelled.

His Lordship's horses had been waiting at every Posting Inn, and the journey had been made easy by frequent halts, while a courier in another carriage containing the servants and their luggage left well ahead to see that everything was in order before their arrival.

"We might be Royalty!" Natalia said in awe-struck tones, at their first stop.

They had been ushered into a private Sitting-Room

by a bowing Landlord and she found upstairs that a maid had already unpacked one of her trunks and a valet was attending to her father.

"His Lordship is extremely considerate," the Reverend Adolphus agreed.

"He thinks of everything!" Natalia said softly.

She had walked across the panelled room to touch a huge vase of fresh flowers that were arranged on a table.

In front of them lay Lord Colwall's visiting card, and she found the same attention waiting for her everywhere they stayed.

Each time she admired the flowers she felt that they had a special message for her and she treasured the cards, placing them carefully in her bag.

'Could any man be more attentive to his future bride?' Natalia asked herself.

Lord Colwall had sent not only his carriages, his horses and his servants to Pooley Bridge.

A week before Natalia was due to set out on the journey a trunk had arrived containing new gowns and for the journey a cloak lined with fur!

"Ermine, Mama!" Natalia had exclaimed. "I cannot believe it!"

She was so overcome by the magnificence of the gift that she had not noticed the strange expression on her mother's face.

Lady Margaret had already been informed that Natalia's trousseau from a Bond Street dressmaker would be waiting for her when she arrived at the Castle.

Lord Colwall had written:

"It will not be possible for you to buy in the North the type and variety of gowns Natalia will require as my wife. I have therefore instructed Madame Madeleine to prepare what is required. Kindly send all the measurements necessary to the enclosed address."

"I would have preferred that we should provide Natalia with her trousseau," Lady Margaret said to her husband in private.

"Colwall knows we live in a backwater," the Vicar had replied. "And to be honest, my dear, it would be difficult for us to find the money."

His wife's face was still troubled and he added with a smile:

"Natalia looks lovely whatever she wears, but I would like to see her in an expensive gown like the one you wore the first night we met!"

"Given to me by my godmother, but I at least went with her when she bought it!" Lady Margaret exclaimed and then she added: "Of course I am being nonsensical. Cousin Ranulf is being extremely kind."

But the feeling of uncertainty—with perhaps a touch of resentment had remained.

"If only Mama could be with us," Natalia said now, looking out of the coach window. "Think how thrilled she would have been to see the South again!

"She has often told me how much she has missed the green fields, the apple-blossoms in the spring, and the hedgerows which are so unlike our Cumberland walls."

"It is a bitter disappointment to your mother that she could not see you married."

"Poor Mama, she cried when we left!" Natalia exclaimed with a soft note of sympathy in her voice. "I felt like jumping out of the carriage and sending His Lordship a message to say that, like other brides, I wished to be married from my own home."

"Lord Colwall had not anticipated that your mother would break her ankle just a week before we were due to go South," the Vicar said.

"No, of course not," Natalia agreed, "and, as Mama herself said, it was too late then to alter all the plans."

All the same, there was an ache in her heart as she knew how desperately disappointed her mother had felt at being left behind.

"Never mind," Lady Margaret had said bravely, "I will look after the Parish for your father and at least everything will be ready for him on his return. I shall miss him, as I shall miss you, darling."

Natalia knew this was the truth. Her father and mother loved each other dearly and it was hard for them to be parted, even for a night.

She was well aware that they would both suffer from what would seem a very long time before the Vicar could travel to Herefordshire for her wedding and return to Pooley Bridge.

Natalia had always thought that her home at the end of the Lake of Ullswater was the most beautiful place in the world.

She looked every morning from her bed-room window towards the mountain peaks high on either side of the silver water—their bare, rugged tops silhouetted against the sky.

They always seemed to her to be filled with mystery and a strange enchantment that was part of her dreams.

When she had learned that she was to be married at Lord Colwall's home rather than her own, she had felt a pang of disappointment.

She had thought of him so often that somehow he had become part of the mountains and the beauty of the lake. It was hard to think of him elsewhere.

Although her mother had frequently described to her the wonder and the majesty of the Castle, she found herself always visualising Lord Colwall as she had first seen him.

He had walked towards her through the morning mist rising over the lake. The mountains behind him had made it seem as if he emerged from the insubstantial mystery of her dreams into the reality of her life.

It had been one of those days when everything was very still.

The mountains which round Ullswater changed colour hour by hour had been almost purple, and the sun was attempting to break through the clouds and glint spasmodically on the silver of the lake.

Natalia, who had been visiting a cottage on the outskirts of the village, was returning home. The basket on her arm was empty of the sustaining soup and homemade jam which her mother had sent to an invalid.

Then in front of the Vicarage she had seen a very

grand travelling carriage and the four horses which drew it had made her gasp with astonishment.

She walked towards them and then a man who had been standing at the edge of the lake turned from his contemplation of it and moved into the road.

Natalia was so surprised at his appearance that she stood quite still under a tree staring at him. Never in her whole life had she ever seen anyone so handsome or indeed so awe-inspiring.

A cape swung from his shoulders, his dark head was bare because he carried his high hat in his hand.

She watched him wide-eyed but, deep in his thoughts, it appeared he did not see her and he walked directly past her towards the horses.

She thought that he was about to enter the carriage, but instead to her surprise the footman opened the gate to the Vicarage for him.

'Whoever the stranger may be,' Natalia thought to herself, 'he has come to see Papa.'

Still without moving, she watched the footman, the crested gilt buttons on his livery glinting as he hurried ahead of his master to rap sharply on the Vicarage door.

'Who can this visitor be?' Natalia wondered.

Then she realised that the sensible thing to do would be to go home and find out.

She had in fact run back to the Vicarage, entering not through the front door but by the back way to deposit her empty basket in the kitchen. Then she slipped upstairs to change her dress.

At fifteen she had few dresses and there was therefore little choice. But she put on the blue cotton with its full skirt and satin sash that she wore on Sundays, and tidied her hair.

Anxiously she peeped through her bed-room window to see if the horses were still outside.

She was overwhelmed with curiosity, but at the same time she felt a sudden shyness at the thought of speaking to a man who was so impressive, of such obvious importance, and at the same time so handsome.

'Perhaps after all, he is not real,' she told herself, 'but just someone of whom I have dreamt.'

She smiled as she recalled how often her mother had rebuked her for letting her imagination run away with her, and for peopling the world with the heroes about whom she had read in her father's books.

Always it seemed to her that the Gods and Goddesses of Mount Olympus resided on the mountains that she could see at the end of the lake.

Sometimes as she wandered through the woods which bordered the water, she thought that she saw Apollo pursuing Daphne, or Persephone coming back with the first stirring of spring from the darkness of the Underworld.

"It is all very well for you to stuff the child's head with these mythical characters," Lady Margaret said once to her husband, "but she has to concern herself with Mrs. Warner's rheumatism and Johnny Lovell's measles!

"It really does not help for her to imagine that she is Mercury, the Messenger of the Gods, instead of just little Natalia Graystoke!"

Her father had laughed but had continued to relate to Natalia the legends that he loved and to teach her about Alexander the Great, the Philosophers of Ancient Greece and the achievements of men like Hannibal.

So when Natalia finally met Lord Colwall, his handsome face stirred a chord deep in her memory and she knew who he was.

He was not one of the Gods of Olympus nor one of the great Conquerors of History.

But just as surely as if a voice had spoken to her from the sky, she knew he was to her someone very special and very personal.

He was in fact her Knight.

Chapter Two

It was of course the Reverend Adolphus who had put the idea into Natalia's head.

She had been twelve years old and was walking with her father along the side of the lake. They wended their way through the silver birch trees which were just coming into bud.

A strong wind was blowing the waters into silver ripples and the clouds were heavy on the tops of the mountains.

But Natalia could only listen enthralled to the story her father was telling her about the Crusaders.

It was one of his favourite subjects, and because he had a Scholar's command of words he could make her feel the excitement which fired the noblemen of England and other Christian countries when they decided they must defend the Holy City of Jerusalem from the infidels.

Natalia used to imagine crowds of men assembling in the Castles of their Liege Lords.

There, inspired with the desire and the will to go on the long and dangerous journey, they left behind them their wives, families and everything familiar.

She could visualise the ships setting out in style filled with horses and men, flying pennants and bedecked with flags.

Their Commander, King Richard the Lion-Hearted, led the British contingent on what must have seemed to many a hopeless mission.

It was thinking of the courage of those that attempted such a feat which made Natalia's eyes shine and her blood quicken as she learnt how much over the centuries they had achieved.

Her father told her about the hospital in Jerusalem which had been founded more than a hundred years earlier to care for Christian pilgrims.

He told her how the Knights Hospitallers had been driven out first to Rhodes and from there to Malta.

He described their ceaseless fight from that small island against the Barbary pirates who infested the Mediterranean and who held at one time more than twenty-five thousand Christian prisoners in Algiers alone.

He made Natalia see as clearly as if she had been there the magnificent Auberges built in Rhodes and Malta to house the Knights of each country, men not only of great courage, but of culture, intelligence and breeding.

Then the Reverend Adolphus had said sadly:

"Napoleon overran Malta sixteen years ago, dispersed the Knights and stole all the treasures they had accumulated over the centuries."

"Oh, Papa! But they cannot be vanquished forever!" Natalia exclaimed in concern.

"Certainly not forever," her father replied. "The Order still exists in other European countries and the ideals they stood for and the bravery which has lifted mens' hearts all through the ages will survive."

"I am glad!" Natalia cried. "I could not bear all that wonderful courage to be wasted."

"That could never happen," the Reverend Adolphus remarked. "Never forget, my dearest, the desire to combat the forces of evil is something which should animate us all."

Natalia considered what he had said, then she asked quietly:

"You mean, Papa, that we should each of us fight physically and mentally against what we think is wrong."

"And for what we believe is right," the Reverend Adolphus added. "I often think, Natalia, that we are too prone to accept conditions as they are instead of trying to improve them."

He sighed and Natalia said:

"But Papa, you have often said in Church that we must love our enemies."

"Love does not mean accepting what is wrong or refraining from punishing ill-doers," her father replied. "We have to be strong in ourselves, to be upright, and above all, courageous, as the Knights were."

He paused and added with a faint smile:

"I often think that when we tell children that they have a guardian angel to watch over them, we give them the wrong image."

"And what is the right image, Papa?"

"I think that instead of an angel, soft and gentle with white wings," the Reverend Adolphus had replied, warming to his theme, "that we each of us have a special Knight who fights on our behalf against evil and all the dangers that encompass us."

"A Knight!" Natalia echoed softly.

"Yes, indeed," her father went on, "a Knight with a sword in his hand! For love is not only a sentimental and romantic emotion; it is also an unsheathed sword that must thrust its way to victory."

After that Natalia was never afraid when she walked through the woods alone or sometimes had to find her way home blindly through the thick mist which would rise unexpectedly from the lake.

She believed that her Knight—her guardian Knight—was with her, accompanying her and watching over her. Sometimes she would even talk to him and sense rather than hear his answers.

So when she was summoned to the Drawing-Room to meet the tall, handsome stranger whom her mother introduced as a relative, she recognised him!

'No wonder,' she thought to herself after her very first glance at Lord Colwall, 'he seems familiar.'

He was just as she had visualised her Knight would look.

As she stared up at him, her eyes very large in her small pointed face, she had seen not the elegance of his fashionable clothes, nor the crisp whiteness of his frilled cravat, but a shining armour, a plumed helmet and a naked sword in his hand.

"This is Natalia, Cousin Ranulf," she heard her mother say. "She is fifteen, and she is our only child, but even so, we try not to spoil her."

It seemed to Natalia that Lord Colwall looked at her surprisingly searchingly. She felt as if his eyes penetrated deep into her very heart.

She curtsied, then found it impossible to look away from him, or even to drop her eyes modestly as she knew she should do. Never had she imagined that any man could be so handsome!

"I wish to speak with you and your husband alone," Lord Colwall remarked abruptly to Lady Margaret.

Her mother turned towards Natalia.

"I am sure, darling, you have something to occupy you in the Study. I will call you before His Lordship leaves so that you may say good-bye."

With an effort, Natalia found her voice.

"May I please," she asked, speaking to Lord Colwall, "go and look at your horses?"

"You like horses?" he asked.

"I love them!"

"Then I will send you one."

She stared at him in astonishment.

"You will send me a horse?" she questioned. "One like those you have outside?"

"A better one."

She had gone from the room, her head in a whirl, hardly believing that she could have heard him aright.

When a month later, the horse arrived, it had only confirmed her conviction that Lord Colwall was the Knight who had been sent to look after her, to guard her and to bring her an almost inexpressible happiness.

Her father and mother had not told her for two years that her future had been decided that afternoon when Lord Colwall had come so unexpectedly to the Vicarage.

She only knew that her whole life had changed.

From having a few lessons a week with old Miss

Grimsdown who lived in the village and who had long retired from teaching, her days were now filled with visiting teachers, two of whom came from as far away as Penrith.

There was a French teacher who spoke with a Parisian accent, which her mother considered most important. There were teachers for Arithmetic, Algebra, Geometry, Geography, the fundamental rules of English grammar, and Music.

There was a teacher of Latin who thought her father's methods were hopelessly out of date and who made what had been a joy and an interest into hours of laborious boredom.

The Vicar, however, had been insistent upon one thing; he and no-one else should teach his daughter History and the Classics, and it was these lessons which Natalia prized above all others.

She did, however, try to learn from the other teachers because, although nothing had been said, she sensed that this new tuition was connected with Lord Colwall and she wanted, above all things, to please him.

"How could anybody be more kind than to give me you as a present?" she asked her horse.

He was a high-spirited three-year-old who had arrived at the Vicarage complete with a groom to look after him.

Inevitably Natalia christened him "Crusader," and sometimes she thought that she herself was embarking on a special crusade. Whom she was fighting or for what cause, she was not quite certain!

"How can we afford all these expensive things, Mother?" she asked her mother once, and was surprised when Lady Margaret did not reply immediately.

"Someone is helping your father and me in this matter," she said at length a little evasively.

Natalia said no more. She had felt sure without being told who that someone was, and when eventually her mother told her the truth, it was what she had always suspected.

Only one person could have thought of her well-being, or cared enough to plan her education.

'I must work hard so that he will be proud of me,' she told herself when she first started on the new regime.

When finally she reached her seventeenth birthday and her mother told her that all this preparation was because Lord Colwall wished, when she was old enough, to marry her, she knew she had worked because she loved him.

She loved him because from the very moment she first saw him she had been sure he was the Knight who had been in her thoughts and her dreams for over three years.

She loved him for his thought of her, for the trouble he had taken in planning her education, and most of all because he had given her Crusader.

"His Lordship told us when he came here," Lady Margaret had said in a hesitant, worried voice, "that when you were old enough, he desired to make you his wife."

Natalia did not answer. It seemed as if the small room in the Vicarage was suddenly filled with a golden unearthly light.

She could feel her heart beating loudly in her breast and yet she could not speak, could not find the words in which to answer her mother.

"Of course, darling," Lady Margaret was saying, "when you meet him again, you may not care for His Lordship. In which case Papa and I would have to explain that despite all he had done, a marriage between you was not possible."

Still Natalia did not speak, and after a moment Lady Margaret went on:

"But if it was not against your wishes, it would be in fact the sort of marriage I had always hoped and prayed you might make. It would be wonderful for me that you should live in the house I always loved and which as a girl was the most exciting place I ever visited."

"You have often . . . spoken of the . . . Castle, Mama," Natalia managed to say.

"It is so magnificent—a dream Castle," Lady Margaret said. "Of course Cousin Ranulf's mother was dead, but his widowed Aunt, Lady Blestow, always played hostess when there were visitors.

"We had very gay parties at Christmas and in the summer. There was a great Ball-Room where we could dance until the early hours of the morning, and lovely gardens where there were endless amusements for young people."

"You have told me about it very often, Mama," Natalia said in a faraway voice.

"I never dreamt in those days my daughter would ever live there! But even so, Natalia, Papa and I have talked it over and we would not compel you to do anything you do not wish to do."

"But I do wish to marry Lord Colwall," Natalia said, feeling as if the words came winging from the depths of her heart.

"I had hoped," Lady Margaret continued, "that he would visit us again, but perhaps it is best for him to wait until you are grown up. He will see then how much you have altered since he first saw you, and I know he will be interested, Natalia, to discover how talented you are."

She gave a little laugh.

"Your Papa has always said that if you had been a boy, he is certain that you would have done very well at Oxford and gained a degree."

"When can I be ... married, Mama?"

There was a note of impatience in Natalia's tone, and now her mother saw that her eyes were shining as if a light had been lit behind them.

"I do not know exactly, Natalia," she replied. "I write to His Lordship every month telling him of your prowess. I know when he came here he spoke of waiting until you were eighteen. That will mean another year at least, and I can assure you that Papa and I are in no hurry to lose you."

"No, of course not, Mama," Natalia said, almost as if it was expected of her. "At the same, if I have only a year before I am married, then there is so much more I must learn; so much I must read. Oh, dear! How shall I get it done?"

Lady Margaret gave her a fond smile.

"I do not think, Natalia, that Lord Colwall will marry you entirely for your intellectual abilities. At the same time your Papa has always said that women should be educated as well as men. I must say I have often regretted that I cannot follow his more erudite arguments, or understand everything he tries to impart to me."

Natalia had bent to kiss her mother's cheek.

"Papa thinks you are perfect, Mama," she said fondly, "and I hope that His Lordship will find me as agreeable."

Lady Margaret gave a little sigh.

"I am sure he will, darling," she said, but she sounded almost as if she convinced herself rather than her daughter.

Because she was so anxious to shine in Lord Colwall's eyes Natalia persuaded her father to take not only the *Morning Post* but also *The Times*.

"I shall never have time to read two newspapers, Natalia," the Reverend Adolphus protested.

"But I have!" Natalia answered. "I must be up to date, Papa, with what is happening in the world outside."

She gave a little sigh.

"Pooley Bridge is so isolated that we might be living on an island in the Atlantic."

"Now, Natalia, that is not fair," her father protested. "You and your mother visit Penrith at least once a month and there are some very agreeable people in the neighbourhood, including my own family."

"Yes, I know, Papa, and I am not complaining," Natalia answered, "but I wish that Lord Colwall had thought it part of my education that I should go to London or perhaps even to Europe!"

She paused and said:

"Can you imagine, Papa, what it would be like to see Rome, or Athens?"

"I am sure your husband will take you to both these places when you are married," the Vicar answered. "It would be disappointing for him if you had seen them already with someone else."

A little shadow cleared from Natalia's face.

"Yes, of course, that is what His Lordship intends," she said. "How clever of you, Papa, to realise it. And naturally I would much rather go with him than with anyone else in the world.

"But you must tell me the whole history of the Colosseum, the Forum, and Acropolis and the Parthenon, in case however clever His Lordship may be, he does not know as much as you."

"I am sure he will know a great deal more," the Reverend Adolphus declared modestly.

At the same time he dropped a light kiss on his daughter's hair.

"But however interesting the Ancient World may be," Natalia went on, "and you know how much their histories delight you and me, Papa, I must also be knowledgeable on current affairs."

There was a little frown between her eyes as she said:

"There are more letters in *The Times* today about the cruelty of very young children being employed in the mines. I think you should read them, Papa."

"I will, indeed," the Reverend Adolphus replied. "I suppose they have not published my letter about the iniquity of 'Strappers' being used to whip into wakefulness the children who labour on the looms."

"It has not appeared yet," Natalia answered, "but there is a letter from Lord Lauderdale insisting that climbing boys are essential if chimneys are to be cleaned, and that people who say it is cruel to use children of five or six years old are talking rubbish!"

The Reverend Adolphus gave a snort of sheer fury.

"Lord Lauderdale should be thrust up a chimney himself!" he declared, "I only wish I could meet His Lordship and tell him what I think of him."

He spoke so violently that Natalia gave a little laugh.

"Oh, Papa, I love you in your militant mood," she exclaimed. "If you only could be in the House of Lords I really believe that you would rout Lord Lauderdale!"

As she spoke she remembered that Lord Colwall was a member of the Upper House.

She wondered why she had never seen his name amongst those who spoke on the subjects which intrested her and her father, and on which they both felt so intensely.

Journeying now in the Dritchka chariot on the last day of their journey as they passed through the fruitful vale of Evesham, Natalia said almost triumphantly:

"There has been no talk in the newspapers of agricultural trouble in Herefordshire."

"No, I have noticed that," her father replied. "It started early last month in Kent and then spread into Sussex and Hampshire."

"There has been a great deal about the Dorchester labourers in *The Times*," Natalia said. "The men are receiving only 7 shillings per week, but they used no violence beyond breaking up a number of threshing machines."

"I read that," her father said. "They behaved with restraint and actually said: 'We do not intend to hurt the farmer but we are determined that we shall have more wages.' "

"Nevertheless, two of the men were sentenced to death," Natalia said in a low voice.

"It is disgraceful," the Vicar said angrily, "when a man cannot speak up for himself without being tried for his life or transported!"

He pursed his lips before he continued:

"I read the case of one man called Legge who was transported because he was declared by the Prosecutor to be 'saucy and impudent' and to have talked 'rough and bobbish.' "

"I read that too," Natalia said. "Yet his character, which included a testimonial from a clergyman, was said to be exemplary."

"How could they do anything so unjust?" the Reverend Adolphus asked. "Legge had five children whom he supported without Parish help on 7 shillings per week. His cottage was given to him, but no fuel."

"I am sure Lord Colwall would never tolerate such cruelty on his estate!" Natalia exclaimed.

"No, of course not," her father agreed quickly. "But I have noticed that there has been trouble in Gloucester which is not far from Colwall."

"But there had never been one word either in *The Times* or the *Morning Post* about Herefordshire," Natalia said quickly. "I am sure Lord Colwall cannot have a threshing machine."

"Let us hope not!" the Reverend Adolphus said in heartfelt tones. "A landowner near Canterbury wrote that in his parish, where no machines had been introduced, there were twenty-three barns. He calculated that in three barns fifteen men would find good, steady employment threshing corn by hand until May."

"And they make extra money!" Natalia exclaimed.

"A man threshing by hand over the winter can earn from 15 to 20 shillings per week," the Vicar replied.

"It is easy for us to imagine," Natalia said quietly, "what the sight of one of those hated machines can mean to men like that! Are you surprised they destroy what to them is a monster of injustice?"

"I do not think," her father said firmly, "that the labourers over the whole country are getting either a fair deal or a fair hearing."

He added positively:

"You must speak to His Lordship when you are married, Natalia, and see that on the Colwall estate at least there is justice and a living wage for those who work there."

"I am sure His Lordship is most generous," Natalia said softly, thinking of how kind her future husband had been to her.

She could feel the softness of the ermine inside her cloak which had kept her warm against the bitter winds and sleet they had encountered soon after they started on their journey South.

She remembered the gowns of silks and satins that had been sent to the Vicarage at the same time as the cloak.

There had also been nightgowns like gossamer, petticoats and chemises so fine they could pass through a wedding ring.

She then realised her trousseau must have cost an almost astronomical sum of money, and she thought that her mother's quite obvious lack of enthusiasm was due to her feeling that Lord Colwall had been extravagant.

Lady Margaret's reaction was in fact because she considered the gifts had been sent in a somewhat arbitrary manner, but Natalia was overcome by such kindness.

The way they travelled, the flowers that had awaited her at each stopping place, the money that had been expended on her over the years, and above all Crusader could only, Natalia thought, have been provided by a man who was unbelievably generous, in thought as well as in deed.

They stayed the last night of their journey at a black and white Inn in Tewkesbury.

Although she was a little tired after so many miles on the road, Natalia had accompanied her father to the Norman Abbey, which the Reverend Adolphus said he had always longed to visit.

The great rounded arches, the stained-glass windows, and the immensely high Chancel had made Natalia feel that she offered her heart up to Heaven in gratitude for all that was happening and all that lay ahead of her.

As she knelt beside her father, she had told herself she could never thank God enough for the happiness she had known as a child and the happiness that would be hers in her married life.

"Thank You, God, thank You," she whispered, and thought even as she prayed that a voice within herself told her that she was really blessed.

"Tomorrow I shall see him," she said later as she laid her head on the pillow.

She was sure she would be unable to sleep but nevertheless she slept peacefully until the Lady's Maid who had travelled with them came to call her.

" 'Tis eight o'clock Miss, and the Reverend Gentleman has already gone down to breakfast."

For a moment, Natalia could not remember where she was, then she gave a little cry of excitement.

"We shall reach the Castle today, Ellen!" she exclaimed.

"Yes, Miss, and very impressed you'll be with it. They say there's not a Castle in the whole length and breadth of the country to equal ours."

Natalia smiled at her. She had already learnt that Ellen had been at the Castle since she was very young and had in fact been born and bred in Herefordshire.

"I shall see His Lordship," she whispered almost to herself.

"Yes, Miss, and I expect you will find a very grand wedding awaiting for you. When His Lordship organises anything, he always expects perfection."

"That is what my marriage will be," Natalia murmured.

She thought Ellen looked at her in rather a strange manner, then the Maid said:

"I hopes you'll bring His Lordship happiness, Miss. From all I hears he was hard done by in the past, and it's only right he should be happy the second time."

Natalia did not reply.

The thought of Lord Colwall's first marriage was something she had pushed to the back of her mind and which she had not discussed with anyone, not even her mother.

"Cousin Ranulf has been married before," Lady Margaret had said when she had told Natalia the reason for her intensive education.

"He was married!" Natalia ejaculated.

"For a very short time," Lady Margaret said.

"What happened to his wife?"

"There was an accident and—she died." Lady Margaret answered hesitantly.

Natalia had been curious, and yet at the same time something had prevented her from asking questions.

She had not wanted to know. She had not wanted to think that her Knight, the man who was bliss, had ever belonged to another woman.

It had seemed to her as if for a moment some of the light that illuminated the room when her mother had told her of Lord Colwall's intentions, had been dimmed.

Then she told herself she was being absurd! It had happened a long time ago, he had been very young, and by now he would have forgotten his sorrow.

"Yet would one ever forget someone to whom one had been married?" an inner voice questioned.

Natalia tried to think of herself in the same circumstances and failed.

'Perhaps,' she told herself, 'it is different for a man.'

"There were no children of the marriage," Lady Margaret was saying, "and I am praying, dearest, that you will have a son, perhaps more than one, and daughters, too, who will enjoy the Castle as much as I did as a child."

She said reminiscently:

"It is a wonderful place for Hide and Seek with its twisting stairways, turrets and towers! It has all the things which appeal to a child's imagination."

Natalia had thought of her mother's words that night when she had gone to bed.

Yes, she would love to have children. They would play in the Castle, and she would tell them the stories that her father had told to her. Of one thing she was quite certain—she would have more than one!

It had been lonely having no brother or sister to share her games, or, more important, to whom she could confide her dreams of the wondrous characters who in her imagination peopled the woods and the mountains.

"I long to see the Castle," she said aloud to Ellen. "It is I am sure a very fitting home for His Lordship."

She said no more but allowed Ellen to dress her hair in what was a more elaborate style than usual.

A travelling gown of dark blue cashmere trimmed with frills of taffeta and small velvet bows seemed to Natalia after her plain cotten dresses to be the zenith of elegance.

She had no idea until she wore expensive gowns what a tiny waist she had, that her skin was so white or her hair the colour of Spring sunshine.

"How do I look, Ellen?" she asked staring at her reflection in the small mirror.

"Very lovely, Miss," Ellen replied in almost awe-struck tones. "You will make a beautiful bride."

That is what Natalia wanted to hear, that she would look beautiful, really beautiful for the man whom she dreamed about, and who had become already an indivisible part of her life.

The Knight who walked beside her through the woods. The Knight with whom she had raced over the fields when she rode Crusader, allowing him in her imagination to beat her because, as a Knight, he must excel at everything, even at the games they played together.

Then finally as they drove round the Malvern Hills they had their first view of the Castle.

Natalia drew in her breath.

She did not believe it possible for any place to be so magnificent! Or indeed so dream-like.

The last leaves of October were still russet and golden on the trees which surrounded it. The great towers emerged above them, grey and stalwart, and the afternoon sunlight seemed to touch the stone walls with a shimmer of fairy gold.

"Look, Papa. The Castle!"

Natalia could hardly breathe the words, and the Reverend Adolphus, who had been sleeping in a corner of the carriage, raised himself to look out of the window.

"Yes, indeed, the Castle!" he exclaimed. "It is a very fine building, Natalia."

"It is wonderful! Glorious! I had imagined it, but it is far, far more magnificent than I thought any place could be!"

There was a river running through the valley below and the Castle, visible for miles away, had been built to stand sentinel over the lush and undulating countryside which surrounded it.

Far away in the distance there were the Welsh Mountains, their barren peaks high in Heaven, purple and mysterious as the mountains at Ullswater.

Now that the moment when she would meet Lord Colwall was near, Natalia for the first time felt nervous.

Supposing, after all, he did not like her? Supposing he had changed his mind in the three years since he decided that she should be his wife, and had found someone else he loved more?

Then she told herself she was being ridiculous.

After all, if he had found someone else, he would not have sent for her. The summons had come immediately after her eighteenth birthday, so perhaps, like her, he had been counting the days until he considered her old enough to be his Bride.

"Do I look . . . all right, Papa?"

The words were a little frightened and the large grey-green eyes in the small face which was lifted towards the Reverend Adolphus were troubled.

"You look very beautiful," her father replied. "Not as beautiful as your mother was when I first saw her! No-one could be as beautiful as that! But lovely in your own way."

"Thank you, Papa," Natalia gave him a little smile, and then bending forward she laid her cheek for a moment against his arm.

"I shall miss you, Papa, and I shall miss more than I can tell you, our talks, our discussions and the clever way you explain everything to me."

"Your husband will talk to you now," the Reverend Adolphus said. "You are not only beautiful, my dearest, but you are very intelligent. It is unusual amongst women, and because God has blessed you, especially as regarding your talents, you must not hide them under a bushel."

"I will try not to do that, Papa."

"At the same time," the Reverend Adolphus said quickly, "no man wants a woman to be assertive, dictatorial, or—shall we say?—bossy. You must be subservient to your husband in everything and do what he says.

"But I would not wish you, Natalia, to waste your powers of intellectual perception, and I feel sure that in the life that lies ahead of you, such qualities can be utilised."

"If in no other way," Natalia replied with a smile, "I should have to be intelligent before I could run a place as big as the Castle!"

"I am sure His Lordship has a very adequate staff," her father replied.

Then he added:

"But you are right, my dear. There will be many things you can do to help your husband to keep the background of his life running smoothly. At the same time, I am sure you can persuade him to use his influence to help those unfortunates about whom we have so often spoken."

"The children, the labourers, the chimney boys," Natalia exclaimed. "There are so many of them!"

She gave a little sigh.

"You cannot expect to work miracles overnight," her father warned. "But a man who loves his wife listens to her. I cannot help feeling that the more people speak out, especially in the House of Lords, against the many injustices and indeed the atrocities that are perpetrated in this country at the present moment, the sooner we can bring to those who suffer both mercy and justice."

"I will do my best, Papa," Natalia murmured in a soft voice.

"I know you will, dear Child," her father answered.

As if he knew Natalia was feeling nervous, he took her hand in his and held it.

Now the horses had reached the valley behind the Malvern Hills and they were proceeding to climb again up the hill on which the Castle was situated.

Because the leaves were still on some of the trees, they only had glimpses of its magnificence through the branches.

They passed through the impressive wrought-iron gates with great heraldic stone lions on either side, and drove up a long avenue of ancient oak trees rising all the time until finally, when they reached the top, there stood the Castle in front of them, a truly awe-inspiring sight.

Built originally on the site of an older Castle which had been erected soon after the Norman Conquest, it had been the focal point of defence for the West of England against the onslaughts of the Welsh.

Its towers and thirty-foot-high Keep stood dramatically on a great conical mound of earth which had been part of the original plan, while other towers had been erected in the succeeding centuries.

For a moment Natalia felt that it was too magnificent, too overpowering! Then she remembered it was in fact the perfect background for her Knight.

'Where else should a Knight live except in a Castle?' she asked herself. 'How many deeds of chivalry, how many great battles against injustice have been planned within these walls?'

It seemed to her that there was an army of servants waiting to assist her and her father from the carriage.

A Major-Domo in resplendent livery stepped forward to say:

"May I welcome you, Miss Graystoke, on behalf of His Lordship, to Colwall Castle, and you too, Sir."

"Thank you," Natalia replied in a shy voice.

She had expected Lord Colwall to be waiting for them in the Hall which, with its Grand Staircase and high Gothic ceiling, was extremely impressive.

Slightly to her surprise, she was immediately escorted up the stairs past the coloured heraldic beasts on each turn of the marble stairway to a bed-chamber on the first floor.

There an elderly woman whom Natalia felt sure was the Housekeeper, and two other maids were waiting for her. They curtsied and explained that they had prepared a bath and a change of clothing after her journey.

"Thank you. That will be very pleasant," Natalia said gratefully.

It was consistent, she thought, with the consideration she and her father had been shown ever since they left home, and she was glad that she was not to see His Lordship until she looked her best for him.

'He thinks of everything!' she told herself once again.

She allowed the Maids to help her undress and enjoyed her bath which had been placed in front of a warm fire. She was aware that the bathwater was scented with roses and the soft towels with which she dried herself smelt of lavender.

The bed-chamber was a fine room. There was a huge four-poster bed hung with embroidered curtains which Natalia learnt had been worked by the ladies who lived in the Castle during the reign of Queen Anne.

There were French Commodes which she knew were priceless and the ceiling had a cornice of brilliantly painted heraldic devices. The carved Medieval fireplace was surmounted by a huge Coat of Arms picked out in gold.

It was difficult to take in everything at once and Natalia was at the moment concerned only with looking her best for Lord Colwall.

There was no need to unpack the bags that had come with her on the journey, for when the Housekeeper opened the wardrobe, it was filled with gowns of every possible material and colour.

"These all came from London, Miss," she explained.

"They are lovely, very lovely!" Natalia said in awe-struck tones. "What must I wear now?"

"It will soon be time for dinner, Miss. I have chosen, if it meets with your approval, a white gown trimmed with Venetian lace."

"You are sure that is the most becoming?" Natalia asked, a worried expression in her eyes.

"I am sure you would look lovely in anything, Miss," the Housekeeper replied. "But I felt that this particular gown was most suitable for this evening. There will be His Lordship and Sir James Parke to dinner besides yourself and your Reverend father."

Natalia smiled. It was perfect that they should be such a small party and she was sure that the reason Lord Colwall had arranged it this way was so that they could have a chance to get to know each other.

But then the Housekeeper went on:

"After dinner, there will be a number of people from the Estate arriving whom His Lordship will present to you. The Agent, the farm managers and some of the more important tenants."

"Of course I should like to meet them," Natalia answered.

She suppressed a feeling of regret that she would not after all be able to talk alone with her future husband.

"Your wedding, Miss, will be exactly the same as the one which took place here in Medieval times," the Housekeeper continued. "His Lordship discovered the details in a book. The food will be the same, the Orchestra will use the same type of instruments that were played here in the Castle hundreds of years ago."

She looked at Natalia's surprised face and said:

"His Lordship is a great one for tradition, Miss. I heard him say that he had searched through all the archives of the family history to find a previous occasion on which a marriage of an owner of the Castle had taken place here."

Natalia did not know why, but the idea that it was all being copied from the past and was not something planned just for her was a little depressing.

Then she told herself she was being nonsensical.

This is why Lord Colwall had wished her to journey to the Castle. It was unthinkable that with his vast possessions and great importance he should be married at Pooley Bridge!

It was completely right and fitting that she should come to him, that their marriage should be traditional and would become in the years that lay ahead another item in the history of the Colwall family.

'I must get His Lordship to tell me all about the previous weddings that took place here,' Natalia thought.

Then with a feeling almost of dismay, she found herself unable to prevent the question which she knew she should not ask.

"Was His Lordship . . . married from here . . . before?"

"No indeed, Miss, of course not," the Housekeeper replied. "He was married from Lady Claris's own home. 'Tis not far away. Only the other side of the hills."

Then as if she felt she had said too much, the House-keeper turned away abruptly to give an almost sharp order to one of the housemaids to hurry up and remove the bath.

With her hair arranged once again in the more so-phisticated manner that Ellen had tried out for the first time that morning, and with her full skirts rustling silkily, Natalia descended the stairs.

Now for the first time she could appreciate the ex-quisitely moulded arches of the staircase, although the marble itself felt cold beneath the touch of her hand.

The huge tapestries hanging on the walls she knew must be of great antiquity and she realised that they depicted battles. Battles in which, she told herself, the Lord Colwall of the day had fought as a Knight.

There were also faded flags hanging on either side of the chimney piece and swords and shields on two walls.

There were a number of footmen on duty in the hall. Their claret-coloured livery seemed very ornate in Natalia's eyes, and their powdered wigs were splotches of white against the dark panelling.

The Major-Domo was waiting to take her down a long Gothic-arched corridor which was lined with suits of armour, some early English and some French. He threw open the door of a large Salon.

Natalia had a quick glimpse of walls covered with pictures, of a ceiling of carved mahogany, of gilded furniture, of sofas and chairs in tapestry and damask.

There were three Gentlemen standing by the great carved mantlepiece but she had eyes for only one!

A Gentleman so outstanding, so handsome, that he seemed, even as he had done in her mother's small Drawing-Room, to dominate the whole room.

Lord Colwall had not changed!

If anything, she thought, he was more handsome than she remembered.

And because she was so pleased to see him, because

everything in her life had seemed to move towards this dramatic climax, she forgot everything, formality, good manners and even her own shyness as she ran towards him.

Her voice seemed to ring out in the silent room.

"You are here! I am so glad, so very . . . very glad to see Your Lordship again!"

Chapter Three

Natalia reached Lord Colwall's side.

She stood looking up at him; her eyes were very
large and shone like stars in her small face, her fair
hair seemed to gleam like a halo in the lights from the
chandelier.

To Sir James Park, watching them, Lord Colwall's
face was entirely expressionless as he said courteously:

"I am delighted your journey was not too arduous."

As if she suddenly remembered her manners, Natalia
sank down in a deep curtsey. Then as she rose she said
irrepressibly:

"The Castle is magnificent! Even more magnificent
than I imagined it would be. And you, My Lord . . .
you are just the same as when I first saw you three
years ago!"

"I was telling Lord Colwall," the Reverend Adolphus
interposed, "how much your mother regrets being unable to accompany us."

"Yes, of course," Natalia said quickly.

She sensed that her father was reprimanding her for
not having mentioned her mother at once.

"It is indeed regrettable that my cousin should have
sustained an accident at such a very inappropriate moment," Lord Colwall remarked.

"It only happened a week before we left . . ." the
Reverend Adolphus began . . .

Natalia's attention was distracted by a big dog which
rose from the hearth rug to approach her tentatively.
It was a mastiff and quite one of the largest dogs she
had ever seen.

"He is yours?" she exclaimed to Lord Colwall. "Just the type of dog you should have!"

"I should not touch him," Lord Colwall said quickly, but it was too late.

Natalia had knelt down on the floor beside the dog and put her arms around its neck.

"He is magnificent, like your horses," she smiled.

The mastiff's tail was wagging and he was submitting amicably to her caress. Lord Colwall watched them both with surprise.

"Herald does not usually take to strangers," he said after a moment.

"That is true," Sir James Parke agreed, speaking for the first time since Natalia had entered the room. "After all these years, Ranulf, he still never greets me with anything but a low growl!"

"Natalia has always had a way with animals," the Reverend Adolphus remarked proudly.

He looked at the picture Natalia made with her white skirt billowing out over the hearth-rug, her bare arms around the neck of the huge mastiff, her face soft and glowing in the firelight.

There was something like a challenge in the Vicar's voice as he said to Lord Colwall:

"I think Your Lordship will discover that Natalia can charm not only animals but also human beings."

It appeared, however, that Lord Colwall was not listening. He moved to the side of the fire-place where there was a table on which were two leather-covered boxes.

He opened them and said in a voice of command: "Come here, Natalia."

She rose to her feet immediately and walked to where he stood. The mastiff, as if he did not wish to part from her, walked at her side.

"I have for you," Lord Colwall said, "the engagement ring which has been in my family since the days of Elizabeth I. It was designed by Sir Francis Colwall for one of Her Majesty's Ladies-in-Waiting, whom he married."

He opened the box he held in his hand and Natalia

saw a large ring, very different from anything she
had expected. It consisted of a huge baroque pearl, set
in gold and surrounded by rubies and diamonds.

"It is lovely!" she exclaimed.

"I hoped you would think so."

Lord Colwall held the box out to her, but for a moment she hesitated.

She had expected him to put the ring on her finger,
then as he did not do so, she slipped it onto the third
finger of her left hand.

"It fits exactly!" she said in surprise.

" I had it altered to the measurements sent to me by
your mother," Lord Colwall explained in a matter-of-
fact voice.

Natalia stared down at the huge ring which seemed
far too big for her little hand.

It was very beautiful and very unusual but it evoked
a memory of her childhood.

She had been about ten years of age when she had
looked at her mother's engagement ring, which consisted of one very small diamond surrounded by even
smaller ones.

"The stones are not very big, Mama," she had said
with the frankness of a child.

Her mother smiled.

"It was all that your Papa could afford when we got
engaged, but when he gave it to me and kissed my
finger before he slipped it on, I felt that every stone was
as big as a marble!"

She laughed and held Natalia close in her arms as
she added:

"It is not the gift which counts, dearest, it is the
love with which it is given. Always remember that!"

Lord Colwall's voice interrupted Natalia's thoughts.

"I have something else for you."

He opened the other box, a much larger one. There
on black velvet lay a pendant which Natalia could see
was intended to be worn with the ring.

It, too, consisted of a baroque pearl—another very
large one. It was suspended from the most brilliant

enamel-work, also ornamented with rubies and diamonds.

As she looked closer, she saw that the enamel rep-
resented a man on horse-back, a spear in his hand, and
the huge pearl was part of the body of a dragon which
he was killing.

"He is a Knight!" she exclaimed incredulously.

"I believe it is intended to portray one of my ancestors," Lord Colwall explained. "The pendant was
made for Lord Colwall in 1655 when he visited Venice,
and every Colwall bride since then has worn it when
she first receives the engagement ring."

"They certainly complement each other," Sir James
said. "You must show your future bride, Ranulf, the
many portraits in the Castle of past Lady Colwalls
wearing both these jewels."

Lord Colwall took the pendant from its box, and
Natalia saw that it was attached to a long, thin chain
which glittered with diamonds.

He held it out to her and once again she wondered
if he would put it around her neck, but it was in fact
her father who did so.

"Thank you . . . My Lord," she said when it finally
lay on her chest, nearly reaching the little hollow between her breasts.

Lord Colwall moved from the table back to the
hearth-rug.

"I think, Sir," he said to the Reverend Adolphus,
"you will be interested tomorrrow to see how a Medieval Wedding Feast can still be produced in modern
times."

"Tomorrow?" the Reverend Adolphus ejaculated in
astonishment.

Lord Colwall did not reply.

"Are you telling me that Natalia is being married
tomorrow?"

Lord Colwall raised his eyebrows:

"It appears to surprise you!"

"I had no idea the ceremony was to take place so
soon!" the Reverend Adolphus exclaimed. "After all,
we might have been delayed."

"I was not afraid of that!" Lord Colwall answered. "My arrangements are made with the greatest precision, and I would have been extremely incensed with my coachman if you had not arrived today at exactly the time I expected you!"

The Reverend Adolphus looked at Natalia.

"My daughter might have been expected to be tired after the long journey," he said. "I should have thought a few day's rest would have been an obvious consideration."

"But I am not tired, Papa," Natalia protested.

She felt uncomfortable at the note of criticism in her father's voice.

"I felt certain, in view of the quite small number of miles you have had to travel during the last three days," Lord Colwall said slowly, "that you would not be in the least exhausted, and I have in fact made all the arrangements for our wedding to take place tomorrow."

"I am quite happy to agree to anything Your Lordship has planned," Natalia said.

Because she felt there was still a feeling of obvious disapproval emanating from her father, she quickly tried to change the subject:

"Your horses are so splendid that you were quite justified in trusting them to bring us here at exactly the time you had planned."

She looked up at him with a smile on her face and added:

"Of all the wonderful gifts you have given me . . . and I have so much to thank you for . . . the best of them all was, of course, Crusader!".

Lord Colwall looked puzzled.

"Crusader?" he queried.

"My horse . . . the one you sent me. I have ridden him every day, and I was going to ask you later if he could be brought here to the Castle. I cannot bear to be without him."

"But of course," Lord Colwall agreed. "That is very easily arranged. When your father returns tomorrow he can carry my instructions to the groom to bring Crusader home."

"Oh, thank you! Thank you!" Natalia cried. "I knew you would understand how much Crusader has meant to me all these years."

She did not see the look at first of incredulity and then of anger on her father's face.

The Reverend Adolphus could hardly believe that, having travelled all the way from Cumberland to attend his daughter's wedding, he was to be sent back like an unwanted servant as soon as the marriage had taken place.

Then with a Christian-like forbearance he realised that it would be embarrassing for Natalia if he were to protest.

As if Sir James realised what was passing through his mind, he tactfully drew the Vicar on one side to show him a collection of exceptionally fine snuff-boxes which stood on a table at one side of the room.

For a moment they were out of ear-shot of Natalia and Lord Colwall, who remained at the fire-side.

"As I have already said, My Lord," Natalia remarked, "I do not know how to begin to thank you for everything you have given me! My trousseau is so beautiful . . . I cannot really believe it is mine."

"Your trousseau is a replica of the one provided for the daughter of the first Lord Colwall when, in the reign of Charles II, she married the Duke of Wessex," Lord Colwall replied. "I found a complete list in our records and I ordered exactly the same number of garments for you."

He paused and added:

"I knew that as far as good taste is concerned I could trust Madame Madeleine."

His words dulled a little the look of gratitude on Natalia's face.

She had thought that he had chosen himself—and with care—the elaborate gowns which were hanging in the wardrobe upstairs; the ermine-lined, exquisite garments which had been sent to the Vicarage.

Then she gave a metaphorical shake of her shoulders.

How foolish she had been to think His Lordship would actually select her gowns. After all, tradition was part of his life. How could it be anything else when he lived in a Castle like this? When he bore a name which was part of the history of England?

She forced a smile to her lips.

"I am so very grateful."

"There is no need for you to be," he replied. "As my wife you must of course uphold the dignity of your position."

She glanced at him quickly, then before she could speak the Butler announced from the door that dinner was ready.

Lord Colwall offered Natalia his arm, and as they walked through the marble Hall and down the wide corridor, she realised it was the first time she had touched him.

She felt her fingers tremble on his arm at the thought.

'How proudly he holds himself,' she thought admiringly.

As they passed the suits of armour which lined the corridor, she knew exactly how he would look dressed in one of them with a great plumed helmet on his head.

The Dining-Room had a high, Gothic-arched roof, but the cold austerity was relieved by the carvings on the stone capitals.

There was a whole log burning in the great fireplace and the walls were hung with portraits of the previous owners of the Castle.

The high-backed chairs were covered in tapestry which Natalia learned later had been worked by industrious Chatelaines over the centuries.

The table was massed with gold ornaments and lighted candelabra, and as Natalia seated herself on the right of Lord Colwall she felt small and a little insignificant in a room that could comfortably seat a very large number of people.

As if Lord Colwall read her thoughts he remarked:

"Tomorrow we shall hold our Marriage Feast here and will entertain over two hundred guests."

"It sounds frightening," Natalia said. "I had always

thought that I should be married in our tiny Church at Pooley Bridge by Papa."

"The Bishop of Hereford will officiate," Lord Colwall told her, "Your father will not be required to take part in the service."

There was a little silence and then, as if Sir James once again sensed the resentment arising in the Reverend Adolphus, he said:

"Have you seen the newspapers today? I read in *The Times* that at Fordingbridge in Hampshire a mob under the leadership of a man who called himself Captain, broke up a factory which manufactures threshing machines."

"Do you think that the Captain in question is the mysterious Mr. Swing?" the Reverend Adolphus asked, diverted for a moment from Natalia's wedding.

"I should not be in the least surprised," Sir James answered. "They say he definitely started the riot. He was apparently on horseback and his followers addressed him bare-headed."

"I cannot imagine why he was not arrested." Lord Colwall remarked sharply. "I hear that the Prime Minister has sent the Seventh Dragoon Guards to Canterbury and the Fifth Dragoons to Tunbridge Wells to quell disturbances."

"I read," Sir James answered, "that Sir Robert Peel has deprecated strongly the action of certain magistrates in yielding to the mobs."

"I can assure you of one thing," Lord Colwall said sternly. "If there was rioting here, which I cannot believe possible, then I would shoot every rioter myself, rather than give in to their demands."

There was something in his tone which made Natalia look at him questioningly.

Then as if he was no longer interested in the conversation, Lord Colwall again began to speak of his arrangements for the morrow.

He went on to tell Natalia about some of the people she was to meet after dinner. She found it bewildering to take in so many names, or indeed to understand what part they each played on the Estate.

'Later I must make a list of them,' she told herself.

But she would not allow herself to be dismayed at the thought of what lay ahead.

She was sensible enough to realise that while they employed two local untrained Maids at the Vicarage, it would be very different at the Castle.

Here she would find herself confronted with over one thousand employees, comprising the hierarchy, not only of indoor servants, but of those who worked outside for Lord Colwall.

She was to meet only the heads of each department this evening, but even they made up a large number of people.

There were the head men in charge of the farms, the dairies, brewhouses, granaries, stables, laundries, and workshops.

There were also the Chief of the carpenters, of the iron-smiths, painters, masons, and glaziers, besides the woodmen, foresters, gamekeepers and those who held superior positions in the garden.

"The man in charge of my greenhouses," Lord Colwall was saying, "is an artist. I think, Natalia, that you and your father will be astonished when you see how skilfully he has decorated the Chapel and how he will transform this room into what will literally be a 'bower of beauty!' "

"You have everything here on your Estate?" Natalia said in awe-struck tones.

"I try to make it a State within a State," Lord Colwall replied. "I am attempting to achieve perfection. I have, fortunately, the advantage of having had very wise and knowledgeable forbears."

He glanced at the pictures on the walls and continued:

"The Tudor herb garden, for instance, is the most famous in the whole length and breadth of the land, and the man who supervises my Carnation House is unchallenged."

"I shall want to see everything when you have the time to show it to me," Natalia said.

"Of course," Lord Colwall agreed.

Dinner came to an end while they were still talking about Lord Colwall's possessions, and when he said it was time for them to repair to the Baronial Hall where their guests were waiting for them, Sir James took his leave.

"You do not require me tonight, dear boy," he said, "and I will therefore, with your permission, return home. I shall of course be here in plenty of time to-morrow to support you."

"Sir James is to be my Best Man," Lord Colwall explained to the Reverend Adolphus.

"I can imagine nothing that could give me greater pleasure," Sir James said, looking at Natalia.

He took her hand in his and held it for a moment.

"I want to wish both Ranulf and you great happiness," he said, "and, somehow, I feel completely sure that you will find it."

The sincerity in his tone was undeniable, and as Natalia curtsied she said sweetly:

"Thank you, Sir James, I know we are going to be very happy."

She smiled up at Lord Colwall as she spoke but he was not looking at her, having drawn from his pocket a list which apparently required his attention.

"Good-night, Ranulf," Sir James said, and then, having bade the Reverend Adolphus farewell, he departed.

Lord Colwall led Natalia through several passages until finally they came to the Baronial Hall.

This had been built later than the original Castle. It was, however, in the Gothic tradition, if more ornate, and was used for all formal occasions including that of making, Natalia remembered her mother telling her, a very attractive Ball-Room.

The Hall was crowded with men who were sitting at long trestle tables laden with food and pewter tankards filled with beer.

There were several great barrels set at one end of the Hall, and it was obvious from the applause when Natalia and Lord Colwall arrived that his guests were enjoying themselves.

Their benign humour stemmed however not only from the importance of the occasion, but also because they had been generously entertained.

Lord Colwall made a speech in which he introduced his future wife, and then, as the cheers of welcome rang out, Natalia went round the Hall at his side.

Man after man was presented to her until the whole throng became nothing but a sea of faces, and it was difficult to hear either their names or the descriptions that Lord Colwall gave her of each person he introduced.

They did not stop to talk to anyone, although occasionally an old man having mumbled congratulations and good wishes would start on a rambling tale of His Lordship's father or grandfather.

It was nearly an hour before the round was completed and Lord Colwall led Natalia from the Baronial Hall back along the passages towards the Salon.

The Reverend Adolphus had not accompanied them and Natalia could not help hoping that, if he had gone to bed, she would have a chance to speak alone with Lord Colwall.

With a little throb of excitement she wondered if he would kiss her.

He had not kissed her finger before the engagement ring had been placed upon it and she wanted more than anything else in the world that he should kiss her lips.

All the way down from the North, she imagined herself being held in his arms; of being close to him; of hearing him say that he loved her and of telling him how much she loved him.

'If only we can be . . . alone,' she thought, and felt herself thrill at the idea.

She knew that he must love her deeply to have done so much for her already, and she thought now that the reason the marriage was taking place so speedily after her arrival, was that he wanted her to himself.

She felt her heart leap at the thought. Of course, that was the explanation.

Even though it might seem slightly inconsiderate

where her father was concerned, she knew it would be a wonder beyond words to be alone with the man she married.

She wanted to talk intimately with him; to know that she was his! She wanted to tell him all the things that she had imagined about him through the three long years when she had thought of him, and of no-one else.

'I love him! I love him!' she cried in her heart as they reached the Salon.

Then, with an undeniable feeling of disappointment, she saw her father was waiting for them.

He rose to his feet as they entered, and before Natalia could speak, Lord Colwall said:

"I am persuaded that you should retire to bed and have a good night's sleep. Tomorrow will be for both of us somewhat of a trial. I am sure you would wish to rest."

Natalia wished nothing of the sort, but she had not the courage to say so. Instead, obediently, she kissed her father good-night, and then turned towards Lord Colwall.

There was a question in her eyes as she looked at him.

'At least,' she thought, 'he might wish to kiss my cheek.'

But he only bowed in response to her curtsey, and she moved away a little forlornly to climb the big stone staircase alone.

She heard a sound behind her and she turned round expectantly. Herald wagging his tail ecstatically was escorting her to her bed-chamber.

Natalia was in fact more tired than she had thought.

She fell asleep almost as soon as her head touched the pillow, and when she awoke it was to see a pale sun struggling through the sides of the curtains.

'I am sure it is going to be a fine day,' she thought.

Jumping gaily out of bed she ran across the room to pull open the heavy curtains. It was in fact the loveliest day she could have imagined!

There had been a sharp frost during the night and the grass was white, the air crisp and the sky very clear.

Below in the valley she could see a river winding its way through fields that were green, and in the forests there was still the red of the beech trees and the golden yellow of the oak.

'Soon it will be winter,' Natalia thought, 'but now it is beautiful—a perfect day for my perfect wedding.'

It was appropriate that the world should wear a semblance of white on her wedding day. Natalia remembered with excitement the wonderful white wedding gown the Housekeeper had shown her before she went to bed.

"Will he think I look beautiful in it?" she asked aloud.

She was sure Lord Colwall would tell her so, and she felt herself thrill with the anticipation of what lay ahead.

A few minutes later the maids came to call her.

"It is a quarter before nine o'clock, Miss,' Ellen announced. "The Reverend Gentleman is having breakfast in your Sitting-Room next door. He asks when you are awake if you would join him."

"Is it as late as that?" Natalia exclaimed. "I am usually called at eight o'clock."

"I thought you would wish to sleep later this morning, Miss," Ellen replied. "I did look in a little earlier, but you were asleep."

"Well, now I must hurry," Natalia said, "especially if my father wishes to see me."

She paused and then asked:

"Where is Lord Colwall having his breakfast?"

"Downstairs, Miss," Ellen replied, "but of course today you cannot leave your own rooms. It is very unlucky for a Bride to see her Bridegroom before she meets him in the Church."

Natalia laughed.

"Are you superstitious?"

"Yes, Miss, and so is His Lordship. He has given

instructions that on no account must you appear until it is time to proceed to the Chapel."

Natalia gave a little sigh.

"Oh, dear! It is such a lovely day and I would have wished to visit the garden, or perhaps to climb to the very top of the Castle to look at the view."

"I don't think His Lordship would like it," Ellen said.

"Of course I must do as His Lordship wishes," Natalia smiled.

She dressed herself quickly.

It was impossible to find a plain morning-gown amongst the elaborate creations which hung in the wardrobe, but she chose the simplest there was and then hurried into the Sitting-Room to find her father had already finished his breakfast.

"I am sorry to be late, Papa," she said, kissing his cheek.

"It is of no consequence, child," he answered. "You might be expected to be fatigued after such a long journey."

"I think in reality I was just day-dreaming," Natalia answered.

There were two footmen and a Butler to bring her innumerable dishes from which she found it difficult to make a choice.

Then the servants having left the room, the Reverend Adolphus said:

"I want to talk to you, Natalia."

There was a note of concern in his voice which made her glance up at him in surprise.

"What about, Papa?"

"I have been thinking since last night," her father began slowly, "that you are being married at quite an unnecessary speed."

Natalia did not answer. She merely put down the cup she had been holding in her hand, and sat looking at her father wide-eyed.

"Your mother and I had thought," the Reverend Adolphus went on, "that when you arrived at the

Castle, you and I would be here for perhaps a week or ten days before the marriage took place."

He paused to continue:

"During that time, your mother asked me to tell you that, if you wished to change your mind, if you decided after all that Lord Colwall was not the man you thought could make you happy, then you were to accompany me on my return home."

"But why should Mama think," Natalia asked after a moment's pause, "there was any chance of my changing my mind?"

"You met Lord Colwall only once when you were but fifteen," her father answered. "If you marry him, Natalia, you will be his wife in the sight of God for the rest of your life. Whatever you may feel about him later, it will then be too late."

"Yes, I realise that, Papa."

"Therefore I should have wished you to have a chance of getting to know him better," the Reverend Adolphus went on. "As your mother suggested, if you had a week together, or even longer, you would be able to exchange your viewpoints on different subjects.

"You would begin to know a little about each other and be quite certain in your own mind he was the man you would love for the rest of your life."

"I am quite certain about that!" Natalia said in a low voice.

The Reverend Adolphus rose to his feet and walked across to the window.

"I have been wondering during the night, and I have not slept very much, if your mother and I did wrong when we agreed to His Lordships' proposal three years ago, when he said he wished you to marry him."

He sighed.

"I thought it strange at the time, and yet to your mother it was understandable seeing you were a distant relative. Then you were educated and brought up in the way which he approved. Now I am not so sure."

"What do you mean, you are not so sure?" Natalia enquired.

There was a silence as her father did not answer.

"Explain to me what you are trying to say, Papa," Natalia insisted. "After all, look at what Lord Colwall has done for me. Look at what he has given me. Can there be any doubt that he loves me as I love him?"

Again there was a silence.

Then in a strained voice her father said:

"I wish your mother were here. Did she talk to you, Natalia, about marriage before you left?"

"We have talked of little else," Natalia said with a smile. "Mama, as you well know, Papa, was very excited that I should live in the Castle she had known as a child."

"I did not mean that," the Vicar said a little uncomfortably. "I mean, Natalia, did she explain to you that when a man and a woman are married they are very close and intimate with each other, and it is love which makes their marriage either a Heaven or a Hell."

There was a little pause and then Natalia said:

"I think I understand what you are trying to say, Papa, and although I am somewhat ignorant on this matter I am sure that I love Lord Colwall in the way of which you are speaking. I want to belong to him! I want to be very close to him!"

Her voice quivered a little as she spoke.

"You are quite certain, Natalia, that you would not rather come home with me today?" her father asked, turning round from the window to look at her. "We could tell Lord Colwall that his plans are too precipitate; that you would rather wait a few months, perhaps until the Spring."

He looked at his daughter pleadingly.

"Then if you are both of the same mind, he can come to Pooley Bridge and you can be married from your own home as I always intended you would be."

"Papa, how could we do such a thing?" Natalia cried. "His Lordship has made all the arrangements! Think of the flowers in the Chapel; the hundreds of people who are coming to the ceremony and the Medieval Feast. How could everything be cancelled at the last moment? He would never forgive me!"

"I suppose not," the Reverend Adolphus admitted dully, "but I am not happy about it, Natalia."

He walked towards his daughter and put his hands on her shoulders.

"You are so very lovely, my dearest, so very intelligent, and so very sweet. I think it would crucify me if I thought that you were unhappy."

"But why should I be?" Natalia asked. "I have told you that I love Lord Colwall, that I want to be his wife, that I want to be with him now and for always."

A smile lit her face.

"I have thought of him so often," she said, "that I feel I know him just as if he had been with me these last three years. I am sure, quite sure he feels the same about me."

There was an expression on her father's face she did not understand.

He dropped his hands from her shoulders and with a heavy sigh turned towards the fire.

"If only your mother was here," he muttered.

And because she did not understand she did not answer him.

As if he felt he could say no more, the Reverend Adolphus deliberately talked of other things—describing to Natalia the Library which she had not yet seen and which he had visited before breakfast.

He made her a list of the books he had seen there which he particularly wanted her to read.

They talked on the many subjects which had always interested them both, and somehow the hours passed until it was time for Natalia to dress for the Marriage Ceremony.

She went into her bed-room to find the Maids and the Housekeeper waiting for her.

When they had dressed her in a magnificent gown of white lace which was so elegant that it could only have come from Bond Street, Natalia looked at her reflection in the mirror, she felt sure Lord Colwall would approve.

The boat-shaped neckline of her gown was very becoming and showed the tops of her white shoulders.

Her tiny waist was encircled by a sash exquisitely embroidered with pearls and diamonds, which fell into a long train behind her.

There was a sparkling diamond tiara for her to wear on her head over the cobweb-fine veil of Brussels lace, which had been worn through many centuries by Colwall brides.

She looked unreal—a nymph who might have risen from the lake at Ullswater or stepped out from one of the cascades which poured down the high mountains after the rains.

Behind the veil, Natalia herself felt as if she viewed the world through a dream.

But this was really happening! She was to be married—and to the man who was the human embodiment of the Knight, her guardian Knight who had been her protector for so long.

"Thank you, God," she whispered beneath her breath.

The Housekeeper's voice interrupted her.

"I wonder, Miss, if I might ask a very great favour?"

"But of course, Mrs. Hodges," Natalia replied. "What is it?"

"His Lordship's old Nanny, Mrs. Broom, is too crippled with arthritis to come downstairs to see you, Miss. She didn't wish me to trouble you, but it would be a real kindness if you could step up to the next floor and let her see you in your wedding gown."

"But of course I will," Natalia replied instantly. "Show me the way."

She lifted the front of her skirts and following the Housekeeper went from her bed-room along the passage to another staircase to the floor above.

It was quite a long way along corridors narrower than those on the first floor.

The Housekeeper stopped, knocked at a door, and Natalia heard a voice say:

"Come in."

She found herself in what in one glance she recognised as a Nursery. There was a fire burning behind the high grate, there was a rocking-horse standing in one corner. There was the inevitable nursery screen made from scraps and transfers.

Sitting in a chair by the fire-side was a small grey-haired woman with the kind and gentle face of one who has devoted her life to the care of children.

"I have brought you Miss Graystoke, Nurse," the Housekeeper said.

"How kind! How very kind!"

Nanny made a great effort to rise from her chair, but Natalia moved quickly across the room to prevent her.

"Do not get up," she said in a gentle voice. "I hear you have arthritis."

"I have indeed, Miss, and some days it is worse than others. I think, if you ask me, it is sitting here having nothing to do."

"I am sure it is," Natalia agreed. "The moment I have time, I will make you one of the herbal drinks that Mama always makes for anyone who has rheumatism in the Parish. It really does help to relieve the pain."

"I shall be very grateful for it, Miss," Nanny said. "Won't you sit down?"

The Housekeeper brought Natalia a cane chair and then withdrew from the room.

"You were His Lordship's nurse?" Natalia asked.

"I have been at the Castle since I was fifteen," Nanny replied. "At first I worked in the house as a housemaid, and then when His Lordship arrived, Her Ladyship, his mother, asked me if I would help the old Nurse who has been brought in to look after him.

"When she retired soon after Her Ladyship died, Master Ranulf was so happy with me that I was allowed to look after him all on my own."

"He must have been a very sweet little boy," Natalia said.

"He was the most beautiful baby you ever saw!" the Nurse exclaimed. "So handsome, I thought at the time he looked like an angel, and when he grew older, there was never a happier child.

"He may have been the only one but he never seemed lonely, and there was not a man or woman in

the Castle who would not have laid down their life for
him."

Natalia smiled.

"I can see you loved him."

"I still do," the old woman replied, "but it is different, very different these days."

Natalia was silent for a moment and then she asked:

"Why is it different?"

"He were badly treated—very badly treated, Miss. I
expect His Lordship 'll tell you about it himself, although they say he'll speak of it to no-one—no-one at
all."

"Who treated him badly?" Natalia asked—and
knew the answer even as she asked the question.

As if she suddenly remembered it was Natalia's
wedding-day, Nanny pursed her lips together.

"You don't want to be talking of things that happened in the past," she said. "All I would ask is that
you make my baby happy. That's what he needs—
happiness!"

"I shall try to make him very happy."

Nurse stared up at Natalia as if her old eyes were
trying to penetrate the veil.

"You will love him?"

It was a question.

"I already love him," Natalia answered, "and I
know that I will bring His Lordship happiness."

"That's all I ask, God bless you, Miss. May He
bless you both."

The words were said in such a heart-felt manner
that Natalia felt tears prick her eyes, then realising it
must be getting late, she said good-bye.

'If he has been really unhappy in the past I will
make it up to him,' she told herself. 'I will make him
happy! I must!'

Her father was waiting for her in the Sitting-Room
and as she entered he looked at his watch.

"It is time we went to the Chapel, Natalia," he said.
"I cannot believe His Lordship would be pleased if
we are late."

There was some reserve in his tone as he spoke of

his future son-in-law, as if he resented the plans that had been made and the fact that he and Natalia must carry them out.

"No, of course, we must not be late," Natalia agreed. "Do I look all right, Papa?"

"You look beautiful," her father said in all sincerity. "I would have wished above all else that I could have had the privilege of marrying you today, but I promise you one thing—I shall pray for you and, always, that God will bless you."

"I think He has done that already, Papa," Natalia smiled.

Then taking her father's arm, she moved with him across the landing and down the great stone stair-case towards the Chapel.

Chapter Four

"The last guest has left, M'Lady," Ellen announced, returning to the bed-room from the top of the stairs.

"Then I must go down to His Lordship," Natalia said with a lilt in her voice.

There were only been a few people left in the Dining-Hall when she had gone upstairs to remove her veil and tiara and change from her wedding-gown into another dress.

She had said good-bye to her father knowing he was displeased and resentful at having to return to Cumberland so quickly.

She had a deep affection for him, but at the same time she longed above all things to be alone with her husband.

The wedding had been even more wonderful than she had anticipated.

The Chapel with its high pillars and great Gothic arches had been filled with flowers. The altar was white with them and in every window-ledge and against every wall there were clumps of lilies, carnations, gardenias and other exotic blooms from the greenhouses.

There had been a choir of young boys whose voices had seemed to soar like angels towards the Heavens.

The Chapel was packed with all the distinguished nobility of the County, but Natalia moving slowly up the aisle on her father's arm was conscious of only one person.

Her Knight—waiting for her at the Chancel steps!

When they had said their wedding vows and Lord Colwall had repeated in his deep voice: "With this ring,

61

I thee wed; with my body I thee worship," Natalia had felt it was a moment so sacred and so moving that the tears had come into her eyes.

She was his wife! She was his! This was the moment she had longed for for three years!

The Marriage Feast, as Lord Colwall had intended, was sensational and an astonishment to his guests.

They had exclaimed over the glazed boar's heads, the geese stuffed with oysters, the swans garnished with peaches.

There was even a peacock served with its enormous tail spread fan-like to arouse loud exclamations of surprise from the diners.

Course succeeded course, and the gold goblets from which they drank were kept constantly replenished with champagne.

The Dining-Hall was filled with guests, and yet there appeared to be a footman behind every chair. Natalia had never imagined that anyone could entertain in such luxury.

The flowers in the Hall made it the "bower of beauty" which Lord Colwall had promised.

Natalia thought how wonderful it was to find a man who was so masculine in every way and yet had an appreciation of flowers and gardens.

It would make yet another interest that they could share together, and she longed for the moment when they could exchange opinions on so many different subjects.

'Now I understand,' Natalia told herself, 'why His Lordship wished me to be so well educated! He himself seems to know even more than Papa!'

When the feast was over, Natalia received so many compliments, so many good wishes and so many blessings for her future happiness that it was finally with flushed cheeks and shining eyes that she left the Hall.

She first said good-bye to her father and then she went upstairs to change her gown.

'Now the house will be quiet,' she thought as she descended the stone staircase.

In the Hall, Herald, the mastiff, was waiting for her. He had been shut up during the wedding and he ran towards her playfully, glad to be free again.

She put her hand on his head and he walked beside her into the Salon where she expected to find Lord Colwall.

He was not there, so she moved towards the fire-place, thinking she would sit on the hearth-rug and play with Herald until he appeared.

It was then she heard voices, and realised they came from another room which opened out of the one she was in.

She had learnt by now that the Salon in which Lord Colwall had received them last night was called from the Norman days "Le Salon d'Or," and the one beyond it was known as "Le Salon d'Argent."

In Le Salon d'Argent she heard Lord Colwall's deep voice and another which she suspected belonged to Sir James Parke.

'He would be the last one to leave,' she thought, 'because he has so ably supported His Lordship all the afternoon and evening.'

The door into Le Salon d'Argent which was to the right of the fire-place was half-open and as Natalia drew near, she heard Sir James say:

"She is enchanting, Ranulf, the most exquisite creature I have ever encountered! So tell me, dear boy, that you have now discarded all those ridiculous notions with which you shocked me the day before yesterday. You will fall deeply in love with this beautiful girl and live happily ever afterwards!"

"Never!"

The exclamation was sharp and loud.

"Listen to me, Ranulf. Natalia is not an ordinary, stupid Society Chit who will be content with a position at the top of your table. She is intelligent, sensitive and will ask more from life than that!"

"I told you when we talked of it before exactly what I want in this marriage," Lord Colwall retorted. "I require, Sir James, in case you have forgotten, a wife who will give me a son! That is all I ask except that she should be pure and untouched. And this time I have made certain of that!"

"Ranulf, have you looked at Natalia? Knowing that she was her mother's daughter, I was expecting her to be pretty and charming, but nothing so unusual, or indeed so breathtakingly lovely."

"You are very dramatic, Sir James," Lord Colwall said scathingly, "but I assure you that whatever Natalia looks like, it will not affect my resolve never again to love any woman—nor, if I can prevent it, to allow her to love me. There is no place for that nauseating emotion in my life."

There was a pause and then Sir James said sadly:

"I can only pray, Ranulf, that time will make you change your mind, or perhaps Natalia will do that."

"In this instance, your prayers will undoubtedly remain unanswered," Lord Colwall said coldly.

"Then I can only say good-bye," Sir James said. "It was a very delightful wedding and the County will talk about the Feast which followed it for years to come. I hope that gives you some satisfaction."

"It does indeed," Lord Colwall said lightly. "It always pleases me when my plans work out in exactly the manner I intended. Good-bye, Sir James, and thank you for your support."

Natalia stood in Le Salon d'Or as if turned to stone.

She had not moved since she first overheard what Lord Colwall and Sir James were saying in the next room, and as Lord Colwall pushed open the door he saw her.

Her face was so pale that he was instantly aware that something had occurred.

"What is it?" he asked. "What is wrong?"

She did not answer because she felt as if her throat was constricted and it was hard to breathe. Then Lord Colwall realised that the door had been open and she must have overheard what was being said.

"I was talking to Sir James," he said and his voice was a little uncertain.

"I . . . heard . . . you."

Natalia managed to speak the words and now she made her first movement. One small hand crept up to her breast.

Lord Colwall advanced a little further into the Salon.

"It was a conversation that was not meant for your ears," he said. "I feel sure you will understand that whatever I said to Sir James does not in any way alter the respect I have for you."

"Re . . . spect?" Natalia could hardly breathe the word.

Lord Colwall walked to the fire-place and stood with his back to the fire.

"I must commend you, Natalia, on the excellent way in which you received my employees last night and my friends today. I am well aware that it was a great ordeal for a girl brought up as quietly as you have been. But let me tell you that you came through with flying colours!"

He spoke heavily, choosing his words with care. But now, looking at Natalia's white face, he realised that what he said had not impinged on her consciousness.

"I did . . . not . . . understand," she said in a very low voice.

"What did you not understand?" he enquired.

"That all you . . . wanted from a . . . wife was that she should . . . produce . . . an heir."

Lord Colwall made a little gesture of impatience.

"Surely it was obvious? I supposed that your mother would have explained to you that our marriage was advantageous to us both."

There was a silence and then Natalia said:

"Did you really . . . think that I was . . . marrying you simply for your . . . title and the . . . position you could give me . . . here?"

"What else?" he asked in surprise. "We did not know each other."

"But we did!" Natalia contradicted. "You came to Pooley Bridge. You saw me and after that everything in my life was changed. You arranged my education, you sent me Crusader, and Mama wrote reports to you of my progress every month. She told me so."

"It was in fact your mother's suggestion," Lord Colwall said. "But surely at such a brief encounter you could hardly expect to engage my affections?"

Natalia raised her eyes to his and he saw they were dark with pain.

"I thought you . . . loved . . . me."

For a moment it seemed as if Lord Colwall had also been turned to stone. Then he looked away from Natalia's eyes to say harshly:

"How could you imagine anything so absurd? So ridiculous? You were only a child when I came to your home."

"I was . . . old enough to fall . . . in love," Natalia answered. "I loved you when I saw you coming towards me through the mist over the lake. You looked as I had always . . . imagined . . ."

She stopped.

"What did you imagine?" Lord Colwall asked curiously.

"It is difficult to . . . explain," Natalia answered. "Papa said once that instead of an angel to . . . watch over us, we each have a Knight . . . like the . . . Knights of Malta to . . . guard and protect us from . . . evil. In my . . . dreams he looked exactly like . . . you!"

There was a little throb in her voice which was extremely moving.

Lord Colwall took a deep breath.

"This is not what I anticipated," he said. "I think, Natalia, the best thing we can do is to sit down and discuss this matter sensibly."

Obediently, as if she was a puppet that must obey his commands, Natalia seated herself on the edge of the sofa. She put her hands in her lap and raised her eyes to his.

She suddenly seemed very small, very fragile—a waif, rather than the glowing, happy girl who had walked down the aisle on his arm.

"I do not know how much you know about my first marriage," Lord Colwall said. "There is in fact no reason for you to learn the details. It is sufficient for me to tell you that what happened then made me determined never again, as long as I live, to be embroiled in the misery, the degradation of what is called love."

"And yet you . . . wished to marry . . . again?" Natalia said.

"I married so that I could have children," Lord Colwall replied. "You know the history of my family. You have learnt that this Castle has been handed from father to son all down the centuries. I want an heir, Natalia, and that was why I chose you."

"Any . . . woman could have served the same . . . purpose," Natalia said in a low voice.

"Not any woman," Lord Colwall corrected. "It had to be someone whom I would be proud to acknowledge as my wife and who would be a fitting mother for my children. You have both these qualities, Natalia."

"But they are external assets," Natalia answered. "They do not affect me . . . the real . . . me. I would never have married . . . anyone I did not . . . love."

"It is unfortunate," Lord Colwall admitted, "that we could not have this discussion before the Marriage Ceremony took place! But I could not be expected to imagine that a girl to whom I had spoken once three years ago would consider herself in love with me or expect me to love her in return."

There was something almost defiant in the way he spoke.

"I see . . . now that it was very . . . foolish," Natalia said in a low voice.

"If you admit that," Lord Colwall said in a brighter tone, "I think the best thing for you to do is to forget that, by an unfortunate chance, you overheard a private conversation between myself and Sir James. You are my wife, Natalia, and I shall always treat you in a manner to which I am quite certain you can never take exception."

He seemed to consider his words and he went on:

"There is much here which I am sure will give you pleasure. The Colwall family jewels are magnificent. You will not find me an ungenerous husband in every

other way, and I am sure that our children, when we
have them, will make up to you for all the shortcom-
ings of their father!"

Natalia was very still and then she said:

"Are you really . . . suggesting that, now I know you
do not . . . love me, I should . . . permit you to give me
a . . . child?"

For a moment Lord Colwall looked embarrassed,
but he said in an unemotional voice:

"I can appreciate that you are very innocent in these
matters, but you will find it not too unpleasant to
accept me as your husband—in fact, as well as in
name."

There was the slightest twist of his lips as he added:

"I am not inexperienced where women are concerned, Natalia, and I am confident that I can make
our association, if that is the right word for it, pleasure-
able for us both."

Natalia jumped to her feet.

"No! No!"

Lord Colwall looked at her in surprise.

"May I enquire what you mean by that?"

"It means," Natalia replied, "that I could not allow
you to touch me . . . now that I know you do not love
me!"

For a moment there was an expression of anger in
Lord Colwall's eyes, but he managed to say unemo-
tionally:

"That is a ridiculous assertion, as you must well
know. For the moment you are upset, but I have asked
you to forget what you inadvertently overheard. In fact
I order you to do so."

"And you imagine . . . even if I could forget it . . .
that I could delude myself into . . . believing that you
. . . love me?" Natalia asked.

"I have told you that there is no point in our discussing love," Lord Colwall replied. "But let me tell
you in all sincerity, Natalia, that I do appreciate that
you will make me a very charming wife, and I cannot
believe that in the course of a few minutes the love

that you have just professed to feel for me has changed
into dislike."

"No, I do not . . . dislike you," Natalia said. "I love
you . . . although I was mistaken in thinking you love
me. But I . . . cannot give you a . . . child."

"Why not?"

There was no doubt of the irritation in Lord Colwall's tone now.

"Because if we had one without you . . . loving me
. . . then it might easily be . . . deformed."

Lord Colwall stared at Natalia incredulously, and
then as if he could not prevent himself he ejaculated:

"What the devil do you mean by that?"

Natalia's hand went up to the pendant which she
wore around her neck. She felt her fingers touch the
cool enamel of the Knight. Somehow she felt that it
gave her courage.

"Will you allow me to . . . explain exactly what I
mean, My Lord?"

"But of course," Lord Colwall said courteously, the
irritation fading from his eyes. "Will you not sit
down?"

He indicated the sofa again. But Natalia sank down
on the rug in front of the fire.

As if he sensed what she was feeling, Herald came
to be beside her and place his great head in her lap.

She stroked him for a few moments until, when Lord
Colwall had seated himself in a high-backed arm-
chair, she began in a low voice:

"I thought about having . . . children and I wanted
above all else to give you a . . . son."

He did not speak and after a moment she went on:

"When I was coming here yesterday and I saw the
Castle, I remembered how Mama had told me of the
wonderful place it was for the young; a place for children to play Hide and Seek, to run along the broad
corridors and to climb the turrets. I knew then I
wanted to have not an only child, such as I myself had
been, but a number."

She paused and stared into the fire before she said:

"I am well aware that at the moment you are . . . incensed with me for not agreeing instantly to your wishes, but I think when you hear the . . . reason for my refusal, you will . . . understand."

"I am listening," Lord Colwall said.

"I must have been twelve, or perhaps thirteen, when I learned first that a baby could be born out of wedlock," Natalia began in a low voice. "There was a girl living in the village, the daughter of a small farmer, who fell very much in love with one of the farm labourers.

"He was, of course, not of her class and there could be no question of her marrying him. But soon people began to talk of her condition, and I learned from the conversations I overheard in the village that she was having a baby."

The colour rose in her cheeks.

"The man was sent away—no-one knew where he went—and the baby was born the following winter. His mother died in child-birth and the child was brought up by his grandparents."

Natalia paused.

"When Jeremy was three years old, he was the most beautiful child I have ever seen in my life. I remember saying to Papa: 'It seems strange that two quite ordinary-looking people should have such a beautiful child. He looks like an angel!'

" 'That often happens with love-children,' Papa told me.

" 'But Jeremy was born in what everybody in the village calls "sin," ' I protested.

"Papa looked across the lake before he answered and then he said:

" 'When a man and a woman love each other with all their heart, their soul and their body, Natalia, their desire for each other can, I am sure, evoke the Divine Life-Force. It pours through them, and at the moment of conception, they beget a child that is in fact, as we should all be, in the image of God."

Natalia's voice died away. Then Lord Colwall said with a cynical smile:

"That is hardly a part of orthodox Christian doctrine."

"But the Bible says that love is more important than anything else," Natalia replied quickly.

He attempted no further argument, and after a moment she went on:

"Now I have another story to tell you."

"I am still listening," he replied.

"You will naturally understand that I often thought about little Jeremy. As he grew older, he had a sweet character which matched the beauty of his face. I do not think there was anyone in the village, however much they disapproved of his mother, who would have said a cruel or unkind word to Jeremy himself."

"I assure you, most bastards are treated very differently," Lord Colwall said almost harshly.

"I have heard that. Yet I have read much about them," Natalia replied, "and there is no doubt that in history, when Kings and great noblemen have fathered illegitimate children, they have all been reported as being extremely handsome . . . like the Duke of Monmouth, for example."

Lord Colwall had apparently no answer for this. Leaning back in his high-back chair, he looked amazingly elegant.

He had not changed from the tight-fitting, long-tailed, cut-away coat he had worn for his wedding, and his frilled cravat was a master-piece of intricate design. A huge emerald tie-pin glittered in the firelight, and his clear-cut features were revealed with every movement of the leaping flames.

"My other story," Natalia went on, "is perhaps a little embarrassing for me to relate to you, but at the same time I want you to understand."

"Needless to say, I am trying to do so," Lord Colwall told her.

"There was another family in the village. The mother had been widowed when her husband was killed in an accident, and she had a daughter—a gypsy-like girl with dark eyes and dark hair.

"Sarah must have been fifteen when her mother decided to marry again. She took for a husband a rough, uncouth man who worked in the gravel-pits and did not belong to the village. I think he was part-Irish, part-Tinker."

Natalia's expression darkened.

"No-one liked him! He drank and was too quick with his fists to make anything but enemies. Not surprisingly Sarah loathed her step-father!"

Natalia glanced at Lord Colwall.

"Everyone was sorry for the girl. Soon after he moved into the cottage her mother occupied, there were stormy scenes and tales that he was knocking her about when he had drunk more than usual! Then one morning the step-father was found dead in bed beside his wife."

"Dead?" Lord Colwall questioned.

"They had both gone to bed the worse for drink," Natalia answered, "and Sarah's mother had heard nothing during the night! When she awoke she found her husband with a long, sharp kitchen knnife through his stomach!"

"Good Lord!" Lord Colwall exclaimed.

"Sarah had disappeared," Natalia continued. "There was of course a hue and cry to find her and a warrant out for her arrest. Then people spoke of hearing her scream in the woods the night before."

She made a little gesture with her hand.

"No-one had gone to her rescue because they knew that it was the route her step-father returned home from the gravel-pits, and he was an unpleasant person to encounter at any time. But there was no doubt that Sarah had been screaming for help."

There was a little quiver in Natalia's voice almost as if she was fighting against the horror such memories evoked before she went on:

"All this happened late last summer, and then in the spring of this year, Mama, Papa and I rose early as was usual on Sunday morning to go to Communion.

"We walked through the garden of the Vicarage, which, if you remember, is just beside the church.

"As we entered through the lich-gate we saw something white lying on one of the graves. As I looked, I realised that it was the grave of Sarah's step-father, and I could not imagine who could possibly wish to lay flowers there when he had been so disliked."

Natalia drew in her breath.

"When we drew nearer, we saw there were no . . . flowers on his grave but a . . . naked baby. It was dead! Quite dead, and it was . . . deformed! Terribly . . . obscenely deformed!"

"My God!" Lord Colwall said the words almost beneath his breath.

"They found Sarah two days . . . later in the . . . lake," Natalia continued. "She was very . . . emaciated, I am told, as if she had been . . . starved!"

A tear overflowed onto her cheek and she wiped it away with the first finger of her right hand, then dropped her head low so that Lord Colwall could not see her face.

"I can appreciate," he said after a moment, "this tragedy must have been a great shock for you. But I cannot quite see how either of your stories need concern us."

Natalia's head came up with a jerk.

"I cannot make it clearer," she said, "than to tell you that a baby born in love, in or out of wedlock, is likely to be strong and beautiful, while the one born without love . . . may be . . . deformed."

Lord Colwall rose to his feet.

"Are you really suggesting," he asked incredulously, "that everyone who conceives a child without love will breed a deformity?"

"No, of course not!" Natalia answered. "But it may account for the number of ugly, brainless, under-sized people one finds even in wealthy families."

She saw the expression on Lord Colwall's face.

"Papa told me the Ancient Greeks arranged beautiful statues round the bed of a woman who was about to give birth, believing the new-born child would resemble them."

She considered her words before she continued slowly:

"I am convinced that the thoughts and feelings of a mother affect her unborn child. Therefore, as far as I am concerned, because I saw Sarah's contorted, abnormal baby, it would be impossible, if I was having one without love, not to be haunted by the memory of it."

She spoke quietly, but there was a note of conviction in her voice which Lord Colwall could not ignore.

"It is absurd! Absolutely absurd, without medical foundation of any sort!" he ejaculated.

"That may be your opinion," Natalia replied, "but I have seen with my own eyes what can happen when a woman is forced against her will to . . . have a child from a man who has no feeling for her other than . . . lust!"

Lord Colwall put his hand up to his forehead.

"I cannot imagine how such things can happen in a small village," he said angrily. "I thought that you were brought up in a quiet, decent place, where you would never encounter such horrors."

"In a village one knows all the people and hears everything about them," Natalia replied. "After all, they are human beings. They are born, they live and they die. And they love or they hate—just as people do in grand Society."

She added almost angrily:

"I think Papa is right when he says that too many of the noblemen of England think the labourers are just animals."

"I cannot imagine what your mother was about not to protect you from such unpleasantness," Lord Colwall snapped. "Anyway, these abnormalities occur in not more than one case in a million."

"That is not true!" Natalia answered. "The Orphanages and Workhouses are filled with children who have no idea who their fathers or even who their mothers might be. I read the figures that were given in the debate in the House of Commons barely a month or so ago. The Member of Parliament who spoke on the subject said our rate of illegitimacy was a disgrace to the Nation."

For a moment Lord Colwall looked confounded by her argument, and then he said almost grimly:

"We are not discussing illegitimacy, Natalia, but the question whether you will give me a legitimate son to carry on my name and inherit the Castle and my very large possessions."

"I will not pretend, My Lord, that I should not be extremely afraid of what we might produce," Natalia replied.

She looked up at him as she spoke and saw the glint of anger in his eyes.

"I am . . . sorry," she said, rising to her feet, "desperately sorry to . . . disappoint you. I wanted to make you . . . happy and I promised to . . . obey you. But I know this would be wrong . . . very wrong!"

She gave a little dry sob.

"I know it would not be the right way to have a child, and I could not . . . would not . . . take such a risk knowing, as I do now, that you have no . . . feeling for . . . me."

"Now listen, Natalia—" Lord Colwall began, but without waiting for him to reply Natalia had turned and walked across the Salon.

She pulled open the door and left the room before he could even rise to his feet.

"Good God," he ejaculated. "What a coil! What an incredible, unbelievable tangle."

Upstairs Natalia allowed the Maids who were waiting for her to help her undress. As they did so, they chattered of the wedding, of how beautiful she had looked and the compliments that had been paid to her from every side.

She heard them speaking, but the sense of what they said could not penetrate her mind. It was like the chatter of starlings outside the window. It was a sound, but it made no sense.

There were smiles on their faces when finally she was ready for bed. She knew they were thinking that Lord Colwall would soon be coming to her room.

When she was alone, Natalia did not get into bed but sat down in front of the fire.

It did not seem possible that what had happened was a fact, that she was not waiting, as she had expected, for an ardent bridegroom, but would sleep alone on her wedding night.

She knew that Lord Colwall would have too much pride at this particular moment to force himself upon her.

But she wondered whether, if she had not overheard the conversation between him and Sir James, she would have realised when he touched her that he did not love her, that to him she was only a body that would give him a son.

She felt certain she would have known. It would have been impossible for her to love him so deeply and not realise there was no genuine response on his side.

She recalled so many things which might have given her a pointer as to the real truth about his feelings: the manner in which he had greeted her; his allowing her to place the engagement ring upon her own finger; the cold way he had spoken; the fact that he had never attempted to touch her.

'How stupid! How inexperienced I am!' Natalia said to herself. 'Now we are married, how can I face the future knowing that he does not love me?'

She laid her head down on her arms, her long, fair hair falling over her shoulders.

There were no tears in her eyes. It was as if she was past tears and was conscious only of a terrible heaviness within her breast and a coldness which seemed to penetrate her whole body.

All her dreams, all the imaginings of the past three years had crumbled into pieces around her. They were as unsubstantial as leaves falling from the trees outside as winter set in.

'I love him! I still love him!' she thought. 'But how can I endure to live with him, knowing the reason for the coldness in his voice, the indifference in his eyes?'

She wondered now how she could have ever been so stupid as to imagine it was just a reserve. It must be quite obvious to anyone else like Sir James, or indeed, the servants.

Natalia felt not only depressed and dispirited, but also humiliated. She had been so sure of her happiness.

She could understand now why her mother had not seemed as enthusiastic as she might have been about the marriage, and her father's resentment at the speed at which it had taken place.

'How right they were! How sensible!' But she had not listened to them.

She thought how hard it would be to admit that she was wrong. How could she tell her parents, who loved her so deeply, that her marriage was already a failure before it had even started?

Yet to stay with Lord Colwall, knowing he wanted her for one reason and one reason only, would be an agony almost impossible to contemplate.

'What shall I do? What shall I do?' she asked herself, and then almost as if a voice answered her cry she seemed to hear the word "fight."

Once again she knew she was sensing the answer of her Knight to her problem, sensing it so vividly that as had happened before, it was almost as if he spoke to her.

"Fight! Fight for what is right!"

She could hear her father saying all those years ago as they walked by the lake at Ullswater:

"Love is not only a sentimental and romantic emotion; it is an unsheathed sword that must thrust its way through to victory."

In the darkness and despair within herself, Natalia felt a little glimmer of hope.

Could she fight? Was it possible to fight for Lord Colwall and to gain from him the love for which she longed?

Natalia sat very still, feeling the warmth from the fire on her face. In that moment she grew up!

She saw that her childish dreams were hollow, the delusions of an adolescent, the conceptions of a girl who knew nothing about the world or about men.

But as a woman, she knew that Lord Colwall was suffering. He had admitted his first marriage had been disastrous, and she knew now that it must have hurt him to the point when he would allow himself to be hurt no further.

That was the key to the problem—she was sure of it!

"I will fight," she said aloud. "I will fight for his love, and somehow, I will win it!"

She glanced at the clock over the mantel-piece. It was still not very late and she knew if she went to bed she would be unable to sleep until she had learnt the cause for Lord Colwall's rejection of love.

There was one person who could tell her, and she was certain that Nanny, having arthritis, would not be asleep.

Putting on a wrapper of heavy satin trimmed with lace, Natalia went to her door and opened it very quietly.

As she had expected, most of the candles in the silver sconces which lit the Hall and the passages had been extinguished.

But there was still enough light left for her to see her way towards the stairs up which the Housekeeper had taken her to the Nursery.

She climbed them quickly, feeling like a pale ghost flitting through the shadows of the Castle, and she hoped that no-one would see her.

She reached the next floor and, after considering a little, remembered exactly where the Nursery was situated.

She knocked lightly at the door, but there was no answer. After a moment she turned the handle and went in.

Nanny was sitting in an arm-chair in front of a brightly burning fire. There was some crochet on her lap, and she must have fallen asleep while she was working.

Natalia closed the door and the slight sound awakened her.

She sat up in surprise.

"Your Ladyship!" she exclaimed.

Natalia crossed to her side.

"I have come to see you because I want your help."

Nanny looked at her face and in the tone of one who was used to dealing with the problems of children, she asked.

"What has happened? Is anything wrong?"

"Yes," Natalia said frankly. "Something is very wrong and only you can help me."

There was a low stool in front of the fire-place and she sat down on it clasping her hands around her knees.

Nanny made no suggestion of getting her a chair but gave Natalia all her attention as if she knew she was in fact a child in trouble.

"I want you to tell me," Natalia said in a low voice, "the story of His Lordship's first marriage."

"Has he not spoken of it?" Nanny asked.

"His Lordship has said only that it was disastrous and there was no reason for me to know the details. But you will understand that I must know them! I cannot help him unless I know what happened."

"Help him?"

Natalia nodded.

"He needs help as you well know, but I did not realise it until this evening."

"I hoped that you would bring him happiness," Nanny said. "I hoped things would be different once you were married."

"Perhaps they will be in the future," Natalia answered, "but not until I can understand why he is . . . as he is."

"He should not have let you marry him without your knowing the truth," Nanny said.

Natalia shook her head.

"It is too late now for regrets. All I want is your help. Was he very much in love with his first wife?"

"He was crazy about her," Nanny replied. "She bewitched him as she bewitched every other young man in the neighbourhood. And she was wicked, really wicked!"

"I know nothing about her except her Christian name," Natalia said. "Tell me who she was."

"She was Lady Claris Kempsey, daughter of the Earl of Powick, whose home is on the other side of the Malvern Hills."

"So His Lordship and Lady Claris had been brought up together?"

Nanny shook her head.

"Nothing like that. Her Ladyship was five years older than Master Ranulf."

"Five years older!" Natalia ejaculated in astonishment.

This was something she had not expected.

"Yes, indeed," Nanny said, "with all the tricks and wiles of a sophisticated Society lady—and he as innocent as a new-born babe."

"Tell me what happened," Natalia asked breathlessly.

It was not difficult with a little imagination to paint in a picture of which Nanny gave the outline.

Lady Claris Kempsey had been beautiful, wild and completely unprincipled where men were concerned.

She had set the whole neighbourhood by the ears with her behaviour and went to London to gain a reputation which was looked at askance even in the licentious days of the Prince Regent.

She had returned to the country and met Lord Colwall, as he had recently become, when he was home from Oxford before his last term.

It was not surprising he had fallen madly in love with her. She tantalised him, teased him, humiliated him, and gave him half-promises of surrender which merely increased his infatuation.

Then strangely, unexpectedly she had told him she would marry him!

He was as surprised as everyone else, and although Lord Colwall's friends and relations begged him to do nothing so rash, and take a wife who could bring him nothing but unhappiness, he had laughed at their fears.

He was in love as only a very young and very vulnerable young man could be for the first time in his life and they were married only three weeks after the engagement was announced, in Worcester Cathedral.

Lady Claris made a very gay and very lovely Bride but, to everyone who knew them, they were an ill-assorted couple. Not only in age but in temperament, from the moment they walked down the aisle as man and wife.

They came back to the Castle after a short honeymoon, and Lady Claris immediately complained of it being dull.

It was not the right Season to be in London, so Lord Colwall had invited large numbers of guests to the Castle and there were entertainments from dawn to dusk.

Late one afternoon a month after their marriage, the guests from a luncheon party had left, when Lady Claris walked across the Salon to the window.

She wore the long, narrow, high-waisted Empire-style gown which was still fashionable and under which no lady wore corsets, and the sophisticates like Lady Claris no underclothes.

Her figure was silhouetted against the sunshine, and looking at her Lord Colwall exclaimed half jokingly:

"You are getting very fat, Claris. You will have to be more careful of what you eat."

She had turned to look at him, a mocking expression in her eyes, and he had felt as if a cold hand touched his heart.

"Can it be—p-possible?" he stammered. "No, it cannot be, and yet—are you having a—b . . baby?"

"But of course!" she replied. "Why else should I have married you?"

For a moment he could not understand what she was saying; then in a voice shaking as if someone had dealt him a body blow, he managed to ejaculate:

"Whose is it?"

She had shrugged her white shoulders.

"I have no idea," she replied.

Then before he could speak to her again, she had left the Salon, and gone up to her bed-room.

Lord Colwall had ordered a curricule to be brought to the front door, and while he waited for it he hated his wife with such ferocity that to prevent himself from murdering her, he knew he must put the greatest distance possible between them.

Taking only a groom with him, he drove towards London to get away from her, to escape from those mocking eyes, those jeering lips.

Fool! Fool that he had been! Dolt! Slaphead, not to to have realised from the very beginning why she had been in such haste to be married!

Why had he never asked himself the reason why she should have suddenly succumbed to his love-making when he had least expected it.

Then, when he was some twenty miles from the Castle, Lord Colwall decided that having been a fool, he was behaving like one yet again. Why should he leave his house because his wife was unfaithful? Why should he leave her in possession of the Castle?

He would go back and turn her out. She could return to her family.

The arguments that must ensue as to whether he would accept the child as his own could be conducted between their lawyers decently and with formality.

Lord Colwall turned his horses round. They were tired from the speed at which they had been driven, and it took him some time to return.

It was nearly midnight when he arrived back at the Castle, but he was determined that he would see Claris and inform her that he would not keep her under his roof and she was to leave for her father's house at daybreak.

He walked into the Hall and saw the expression of surprise on the faces of the two footmen on duty. There was a cloak and hat lying on one of the chairs.

"Where is Her Ladyship?" he asked.

There was a moment's uncomfortableness before the flunkey replied somewhat hesitatingly:

"I believe—Her Ladyship is—upstairs, M'Lord."

He went up the stone staircase like a man possessed and burst open the door of the bed-chamber.

His wife was in bed, but she was not alone!

For a moment there was sheer unbridled murder in

Lord Colwall's eyes. Then he seized the man who lay beside Lady Claris and dragged him from the bed onto the floor.

He was naked and when Lord Colwall recognised him as an older man of no social importance, someone whom he would hardly have considered worth a glance, he had laughed scornfully.

"I would not soil my hands by fighting you," he said. "But I intend to kick you out of my house."

He dragged the man just as he was down the stairs. The two servants were standing spell-bound in the Hall.

"Open the door," Lord Colwall commanded.

As they hastened to obey, there was a sudden cry from the staircase above.

Lady Claris was standing there. She had flung a diaphanous wrapper over her nightgown, her dark hair streaming over her shoulders.

"Stop, Ranulf!" she cried. "You cannot do this! You cannot behave in such a manner! It will cause a scandal, as you well know."

"You should have thought of that earlier!" Lord Colwall answered.

The man, whom he was holding tightly by his arms, made no appeal. He was obviously struck dumb by what was occurring.

"Ranulf! I command you to let Charles dress and leave decently."

"There is nothing decent about him or you!" Lord Colwall replied harshly.

He dragged the man towards the doorway and Lady Claris screamed furiously:

"Damn you! Will you listen to me?"

She began to run down the stairs.

Whether it was her nightgown which impeded her or the fact that she was heavy with child, it was impossible to determine, but she tripped and fell forward with a shrill cry which echoed round the walls.

She rolled over and over down the uncarpeted stone stairway to land in the Hall at the feet of her husband and her paramour.

Her neck was broken.

Chapter Five

Lord Colwall came down the steps of the Castle with a pronounced scowl on his face.

The black stallion waiting for him was being held with difficulty by two grooms and he swung himself quickly into the saddle.

"Her Ladyship's horse was a bit frisky, too, M'Lord," one of the grooms said, "and I was to tell Your Lordship that she's gone on ahead."

Lord Colwall looked surprised, and then a little way down the drive he saw a figure in a blue habit riding a roan mare and holding it under control with some difficulty.

He set off towards Natalia at a sharp pace. He had not slept well and had risen that morning feeling both apprehensive and angry.

'How,' he asked himself, 'could I ever imagine I would find myself in such an uncontrollable situation?'

At the same time he had to admit that in the circumstances Natalia had behaved in an exemplary manner.

She had neither wept nor berated him as another woman might have done. She had assembled her arguments well and had been logical in the manner in which she had presented them.

At the same time he was appalled at what the future might hold.

He reached Natalia's side and saw that she was wearing a sapphire-blue riding-habit of velvet which accentuated her small waist.

Her high-crowned riding-hat was encircled by a

gauze veil which hung down her back and she looked very young and lovely.

"Good morning, My Lord," she said in a light tone as he approached. "I had hoped that you would invite me to ride with you this morning; but, as you did not do so, I presumed to order my own horse in the hope that I might be allowed to accompany you."

"I am delighted you should do so," Lord Colwall replied.

"And dare I suggest that I race you across the Park, which I feel will blow away some of the cobwebs?" Natalia asked.

She turned her horse as she spoke and rode off without waiting for his reply. Lord Colwall, pressing his top hat firmly on his head, set off in pursuit.

As she galloped ahead of him, he admitted to himself that she rode surprisingly well. He had expected her to be proficient, but himself an extremely experienced horseman he recognised that Natalia was in fact outstanding.

The sound of their horses' hoofs thundered in their ears as they sped across the Park and on through open fields.

Finally, when they must have gone for over two miles and Lord Colwall was two lengths ahead, they both drew in their horses and he turned to see Natalia's laughing face.

"You beat me fairly," she admitted, "as I had always hoped you would!"

He raised his eyebrows and she explained:

"When in my imagination Crusader and I were racing my Knight, I always permitted him to win! I felt it would lower his prestige to be defeated by a mere woman."

"You should not be so modest," Lord Colwall said. "You are, as I expect you well know, an exceptionally good horsewoman!"

"I am glad that one of my accomplishments finds favour in Your Lordship's eyes."

"It will be interesting to discover the others," he replied.

Their horses were walking side by side, sweating a little at the speed at which they had galloped.

"I thought last night that you were extremely surprised to find that I should have a will of my own," Natalia said with a smile. "You had me brought up in accordance with your wishes and then, unexpectedly, I disconcerted you."

Lord Colwall said nothing and Natalia went on with a look of mischief in her eyes:

"I wonder if you know the story that when Adam behaved so badly in the Garden of Eden, God protested about him to one of the Angels.

" 'But, My Lord' the Angel replied, 'you gave Adam free will!'

" 'I gave him free will to agree with me!' God answered. 'But when he disagrees, it is just darned impudence!' "

Lord Colwall laughed.

"Are you seriously comparing me with the Almighty?"

"Why not?" Natalia asked. "You are very autocratic."

"I have a feeling," he said, noting the dimple that had appeared at the side of her mouth, "that you are being deliberately provocative! If you are not careful, Natalia, I shall lock you up in one of the dungeons beneath the Castle, or perhaps incarcerate you in one of the turrets!"

"Oh, let it be a turret!" Natalia cried. "I can then let down my long hair to make a rope by which to escape!"

She glanced at him from under her eye-lashes and added:

"That is if I really wanted to leave . . ."

She touched her horse with a spur as she spoke and once again she was forging ahead and Lord Colwall had to exert himself to keep beside her.

They returned to the Castle in time for luncheon. Natalia chatted gaily all through the meal and when they had finished, she persuaded Lord Colwall to show her his home.

He was amazed at how much she knew about the pictures which hung on the ancient walls and the furniture which graced every Salon.

Natalia had expected the Castle to be impressive. What she had not known was that every owner for centuries had been not only an adventurer, but also a collector.

From the time the Castle had been built, the Colwalls had acquired valuables from all over the world by conquest, by piracy and from the sheer joy of acquisition.

There were scrolls and jade from China; mosaics and carpets from Persia, marble and bronze statues from Greece, pictures by all the great Masters from Italy, France and Holland.

Where the scenes depicted were mythological, Natalia was better informed than Lord Colwall had believed possible. He had expected to be the teacher, but found himself the pupil.

Finally, when they had inspected the magnificent Library which had so delighted the Reverend Adolphus, he unlocked a door which stood in a corner of it.

It was very heavily made. The hinges were of brass and so were the studs which were deeply embedded in the old oak.

"This is my Strong-Room," he explained.

When he pulled open the door for Natalia to enter, she gave a gasp of surprise.

It was a circular room, the windows were only narrow slits, and she realised she was in one of the turrets.

She could see that all round the room there were glass cases, rising one above the other, and they contained jewels.

There was a case in which reposed the magnificent diamond tiara she had worn for her wedding, surrounded by a necklace, earrings, bracelets and rings, all of the same design.

In another case there was a parure of emeralds, another of rubies, another of sapphires, and a fifth containing a diadem of pearls.

In other cases there were amethysts, topazes, turquoises, aquamarines, gold and silver necklaces of great antiquity set with un-cut stones.

Baroque pearls filled a bowl to overflowing, which Lord Colwall explained was treasure trove from the West Indies brought home by the Colwall who sailed with Drake.

There was also enamel work like the pendant which Natalia wore round her neck and which had been made by master craftsmen of Venice, whose work of two centuries earlier remained unrivalled.

Natalia ran like a child from case to case exclaiming excitedly and asking Lord Colwall to explain to her where the jewels had been found.

She listened while he related deeds of daring and sometimes of terror, the Colwall who had acquired them sometimes escaping death only by inches.

Finally he opened the cases and she took out the jewels one by one to touch them, to try them on her wrists and place them against her white skin.

She could see her reflection in the oval mirror which hung on the wall. It had come from India and was encrusted with emeralds the size of pigeon's eggs and diamonds seemingly too big to be real.

"Tell me more! Tell me about this!" she kept saying, until finally Lord Colwall protested:

"I think I have exhausted my stories. If you want to know more you will have to search through the Family Records which contain particulars of my ancestors' journeys and the battles in which they were engaged."

"Perhaps we could put them all together and make a book," Natalia suggested.

She was just going to add ". . . for future generations," when she realised what the words suggested!

Blushing she turned to the nearest case, took out an enormous tiara of sapphires and diamonds, and set it upon her head.

It became her fair hair, and the jewels echoed the light in her eyes as she turned towards Lord Colwall to say:

"Now I look like a Queen, fit to sit beside your throne!"

She was laughing as she spoke, and her voice seemed to echo round the room while a shaft of sunlight coming through an arrow-slit window made the great tiara glitter almost blindingly.

"Why not fit to grace my bed?" Lord Colwall asked.

His eyes met Natalia's as he spoke and somehow it was impossible for either of them to move.

Something passed between them until, as she saw a fire smouldering in his eyes, she took the tiara from her head and put it in his hands.

Then she walked away, leaving him alone amongst his jewels.

The following morning Lord Colwall returned from a meeting that he had been obliged to attend in Hereford.

There was no sign of Natalia as he come into the Hall, nor did he find her in the Salon.

He next tried the Library and had only just walked towards the fire-place to hold out his hands to the blaze, when the door opened and she came in.

She was still wearing a bonnet which framed her small face and the silk ribbons were tied under her chin.

She had not discarded the cloak she had worn, and it was obvious as she moved across the space between them that she was in a hurry.

She reached Lord Colwall's side and stood looking up at him, her eyes troubled, and he fancied in surprise there was something like anger in her expression.

"You have a threshing-machine!"

Lord Colwall raised his eyebrows.

"Why should it concern you?"

"I understand it has just been installed."

"It arrived on the Estate three days ago."

"How can you do anything so foolhardy at this particular moment?" Natalia cried, "and why indeed should you want one?"

"I consider myself somewhat remiss in not having

one before," Lord Colwall replied. "Most estates of this
size have moved with the times. I did in fact intend
to purchase one last year, but I was not impressed
with the performance of the ones I inspected."

"Do you realise what it will mean to the men you
employ?" Natalia asked, and now there was no doubt
that her tone was angry.

"I cannot imagine why it should interest you," Lord
Colwall answered.

"I have just come from a cottage where there are
nine people living on the wages of one man."

"You have come from a cottage?" Lord Colwall repeated. "What right had you to visit one of my cottages
without telling me?"

"I learnt this morning after you had departed for
Hereford, that an Aunt of one of the under-housemaids
was very ill," Natalia answered. "I took her some soup
and food for the children and I found . . ."

She paused as if it was difficult to speak of what
she had discovered.

"What did you find?" Lord Colwall asked harshly.

"I found a household on the verge of starvation!"

"It is not true. The labourers on my estate are paid
more than the average."

"I heard that," Natalia said. "You give them eight
shillings per week. Do you really call that an adequate
sum for a man to support his widowed mother, his
wife and seven children?"

Lord Colwall did not answer and she went on:

"The only thing they can look forward to after the
summer, and their only chance of survival, is by threshing through the winter by which they can earn just
enough to feed them until the spring. At the moment
they are existing on potatoes and roots."

"I cannot believe this is the truth."

"Of course it is the truth!" Natalia contradicted. "I
have read about such things, but I had not seen the
actual suffering myself. Those children are skin and
bones, and the cottage . . . it looks decent enough on
the outside, but the conditions within are indescribable."

"Dirty?" Lord Colwall asked.

"No! Poverty-stricken! They have hardly a blanket with which to cover themselves or a cup or plate on which to eat. Such things cost money."

"I will investigate your allegations concerning starvation."

"It will soon be worse if you bring a threshing-machine into use," Natalia cried. "Do you know what the labourers in other Counties are asking?"

"If you are referring to the rioters, I do not wish to hear," Lord Colwall replied.

"They are asking for justice," Natalia went on as if he had not spoken. "They want two shillings per day for each man and one shilling and sixpence for each child he has to support . . . Does that seem too much for a landlord who owns as much as you do?"

"That is not the point!" Lord Colwall exclaimed. "Let me make it clear once and for all, Natalia, I will not have you visiting the cottages on my Estate. I forbid it!"

"I can quite imagine why you do not wish me to do so!" Natalia answered. "The old woman, the grandmother of the children, told me that the last lady who visited her was your mother!"

There was silence. Then Natalia said in very different tone:

"Please, My Lord, get rid of the threshing-machine! Send it away and tell your men you will not use it."

"Why should I do that?" Lord Colwall enquired.

"Because these machines have caused trouble in every County except this," Natalia answered. "You have read of the riots in Kent and Surrey, in Hampshire and even in Gloucestershire. Surely you do not want them to happen here?"

"I will take good care they do not!"

"And how will you prevent it?" Natalia enquired. "Do you imagine other land-owners have not regretted that their ricks were fired, their machines broken up? And what is much more important, good will between the employer and the employee disrupted to the point of violence?"

"I have told you it is not your business," Lord Colwall said. "I know quite well how to deal with my own men."

"The children are hungry," Natalia said in a low voice.

"I will make enquiries," Lord Colwall promised, but his voice was cold and she knew he was angry with her.

She went from the room to take off her bonnet and cloak before luncheon.

When they sat down in the large Dining-Room, she found that Lord Colwall was deliberately talking of other things.

There was a hardness in his voice and she knew that any progress she might have made in gaining his confidence had been lost because she had argued with him about the threshing-machine.

She felt despairingly that she had lost completely the little ground she had gained, because she had been so appalled at the conditions she had found on what had seemed to her a happy and prosperous Estate.

'What could I do but tell him what I think?' she asked herself.

She knew that it would have been impossible for her to pretend she had not seen the suffering in the labourer's cottage.

She had heard the despair in the women's voices when they talked of the difference the threshing-machine would make in their lives.

'What can I say? What can I do to help them?' Natalia asked herself desperately.

At the same time she longed to put out her hand to Lord Colwall and ask him to smile at her, to persuade him to laugh as he had done yesterday when she had teased him and they had joked together, not only through luncheon but also through dinner.

It had been a cosy and intimate occasion that she had never known before, when after dinner they had sat in front of the fire in the Library and Lord Colwall had shown her drawings by great Italian artists that one of his ancestors had brought from Rome.

There was even one by Michelangelo and several

by Tiepolo, which had made Natalia exclaim with delight.

When finally it was time to go to bed, she had put away the portfolio almost reluctantly.

"There is so much more I want to know. So much more I have to learn about such things," she said.

"You have plenty of time," he answered with a smile. "You are very young, Natalia, but already surprisingly knowledgeable on such matters."

"Thanks to you, My Lord, although it was Papa who taught me most of what I know about Art."

"One day I will take you to Rome."

She looked at him with delight.

"That is one of the things I have longed to hear you say."

"You anticipated I might say it?"

"I have always wanted to visit Italy and Greece," Natalia answered, "and Papa suggested once that you might wish to take me to both countries. I cannot imagine anything more exciting than seeing the Acropolis with you to instruct me."

"It is very beautiful in the moonlight," Lord Colwall said, "and very romantic."

There was something in his voice that made her drop her eyes shyly before his.

Then as if he regretted what he had said he added:

"I am sure you would find the Colosseum equally fascinating . . . One can always imagine the Christians struggling against the wild animals for their lives."

"I assure you, My Lord, that is not at all the type of entertainment I should find amusing," Natalia protested.

"Then we can wait for the moonlight and visit the Forum," Lord Colwall suggested.

She felt he was teasing her, and at the same time she half suspected that he was being charming for his own ends.

He had only to sweep away her defences and then she would be all too ready to acquiesce in his wishes.

Natalia had risen to her feet with a little smile.

"I think, My Lord, we must for the moment concern ourselves with the present."

He took her hand in his.

"May I tell you I have enjoyed myself today?" he
asked.

There was a note of sincerity in his voice which
she could not misunderstand.

"I also found it very entertaining," she said. "Thank
you, My Lord."

She curtsied as she spoke, and then as he opened
the door for her she passed through it without looking
at him again.

She had the uneasy feeling that if she did so she
might throw herself into his arms, agree to do whatever he wanted, and promise not to oppose him any
longer.

'It is going to be hard to be resolute, when he is so
beguiling,' she told herself.

She loved him already more than she imagined it
was possible to love anybody. She loved everything
about him; the sound of his voice, his handsome features, the way his hair grew back from his forehead,
his strong sensitive fingers.

She had only to see him walk across the room to
feel her heart turn over in her breast.

Yet even as she thought about him, she remembered
the tone of his voice when he had been talking with
Sir James, when he had said so emphatically that
there could be no possible mistake:

"I assure you, whatever Natalia looks like, it will
not affect my resolve never again to love any woman,
nor, if I can prevent it, to allow her to love me!"

When at last the Maids had withdrawn and Natalia was alone in her bed-room, she told herself that
she must not be misled into thinking pleasantness was
affection, nor that desire for his own way was love.

Now, because she was determined that somehow she
would make Lord Colwall love her, she knew it was
stupid to antagonise him or incite him to anger as she
had just done.

Yet she thought as they finished luncheon there was nothing she could have done but speak in defence of the men who would be facing incredible hardships during the winter because of the threshing-machine.

"This evening," Lord Colwall said in a distant voice which meant he was still incensed with her, "I have arranged that we shall dine with the Earl of Frome. He is a relative by marriage. His house is only the other side of Hereford so the drive will not fatigue you."

"I should like that," Natalia said.

"It is rather soon after our marriage to accept invitations," Lord Colwall said, "but His Lordship is departing for London the day after tomorrow, and is extremely anxious to make your acquaintance before he leaves."

"It is of course Lord Frome who speaks regularly in the debates in the House of Lords," Natalia said. "I should like very much to meet him."

"Then if that be your pleasure, we will leave here at about six o'clock."

Lord Colwall rose to his feet as he spoke and Natalia led the way from the Dining-Room.

When they were out of ear-shot of the servants and she realised that he was about to leave her she said:

"Please will you remember what I have said about the labourer's family? I will take them some food tomorrow, but there must be many more in the same state who need your help and consideration."

"I have told you, Natalia, that I will not have you interfering in matters that do not concern you," Lord Colwall said sharply.

He walked away and left her standing alone in the corridor beside a suit of armour.

The dinner party with Lord Frome was most enjoyable.

As they were supposedly on their honeymoon, Lord Frome had not invited more than four other guests, and with his own family of sons and daughters they sat down a mere twelve to dinner.

The house was delightful, the dinner well cooked,

and Lady Frome was a kindly, motherly woman who made Natalia feel at home. Her daughters admired unreservedly her gown and her jewels.

Lady Frome had known Lady Margaret and had many tales of how attractive Natalia's mother had been in the old days.

She told Natalia how many ardent and important beaux had pursued Lady Margaret only to be refused when she gave her heart to the Reverend Adolphus and married him despite parental opposition.

There was so much to talk about and so much to hear, that Natalia was quite surprised when Lord Colwall said it was getting late and time they returned home.

It was very cold when they stepped out of the warm house.

There was however a foot-warmer in the comfortable carriage, which had His Lordship's Coat of Arms emblazoned on the panels, and there was a big fur rug to cover them both as they sat side by side against the soft cushions.

'We are in a little world almost of our own,' Natalia thought.

She wondered what she would do if Lord Colwall put his arms around her and kissed her.

Would she surrender herself to him?

She knew she longed above all things to feel his lips on hers, and then she remembered again the cold manner in which he had spoken to Sir James, and knew that nothing had changed as far as he was concerned.

They passed through the centre of Hereford and were just on the outskirts of the town, moving along a road that appeared to be empty of traffic, when the horses were pulled up with a jerk that almost flung Natalia onto the floor.

"What has occurred?" Lord Colwall enquired as he struggled to let down the window.

The footman opened the door.

"I'm afraid there has been an accident, M'Lord," he said. "We didn't see the child until we were right on top of him."

"What child?" Lord Colwall asked.

But even as he asked the question, Natalia had slipped from the carriage and out into the roadway.

The coachman had brought the horses to a standstill, but lying against the wheel she could see in the light of the lanterns a small boy.

She knelt down beside him, and as she did so she heard Lord Colwall say to the footman behind her:

"How did it happen?"

"The child must have been a-wandering about at the side of the road, M'Lord. We didn't see him until the horses were right upon him. We'd have run right over him if Mr. Hempton hadn't pulled them aside just in time."

"Is he dead?" Lord Colwall asked.

Before the footman could reply, Natalia, who was kneeling by the boy, said:

"No, I think he is unconscious but he has a very bad gash on one of his knees and his hand seems to be covered in blood."

"I wonder where he comes from," Lord Colwall said. "Perhaps we had better take him back to the town."

"I think, M'Lord," Hempton said from the box, "that he's a lad from the Orphanage."

"Which Orphanage?" Lord Colwall enquired.

"The Colwall Orphanage which was built by Your Lordship's grandfather."

"Oh, yes of course I remember," Lord Colwall said.

While he was talking, Natalia instructed the footman to lift the child into the carriage. He was laid on the small seat opposite the one on which she and Lord Colwall had been seated.

Now by the light of the candle-lantern inside the carriage she could see he was a child of only four or five years of age.

He had fair hair, a thin, delicate face and was very pale—presumably from the accident. There was a bruise on his forehead where he must have fallen against a stone.

Natalia felt his legs and arms and felt quite certain that owing to Hempton's skilful driving the carriage wheel had not passed over him but had simply knocked him down.

She lay the fur rug gently over the child as Lord Colwall climbed back into the carriage.

"Drive to the Orphanage," he said, "and go slowly."

"Very good, M'Lord."

Natalia was kneeling on the floor of the carriage holding the child on the small seat for fear he should fall off. The light gleamed on her fair hair and glittered on her diamond necklace.

Lord Colwall watched her, but he said nothing as they travelled slowly for perhaps half a mile.

When the carriage came to a standstill, Natalia said:

"The child is still unconscious. We must make it clear that he requires careful nursing and that they should send for a physician."

"I doubt if one will come out at this time of night to an Orphanage," Lord Colwall replied.

Then as a door opened in response to the footman's knock, he alighted.

As if she did not trust him to insist that the child needed urgent attention, Natalia followed Lord Colwall from the carriage and walked up a short stone-paved path.

She saw the building built of red brick was not large and it had small, gabled windows.

"That must have been Timothy in the road-way, M'Lord," she heard the woman say as she reached Lord Colwall's side. "He's always running away to go and look for his mother. He hasn't been with us long."

The woman looked harassed. The apron she wore over her gown was none too clean and there were strands of hair escaping from under her mob cap.

"I am Lady Colwall," Natalia said politely holding out her hand. "I am sorry that we have hurt one of your children."

"There's too many of them and that's a fact, M'Lady," the woman answered. "Over twenty I've got at the moment, and not a soul to help me."

"No-one to help you?" Natalia exclaimed in surprise.

"I think perhaps we should step inside," Lord Colwall said. "It is cold standing here and we have just come from a warm atmosphere."

"Yes, of course, M'Lord, excuse me," the woman stuttered, afraid she had done the wrong thing.

She held open the door while Natalia and Lord Colwall walked inside.

The Orphanage was austere, but they could see the room they entered was adequately furnished, although it was extremely untidy and badly in need of being dusted.

"I must apologise, M'Lord . . ." the woman began, but Lord Colwall interposed:

"Will you tell me your name?"

"Mrs. Moppam, M'Lord."

"And you have been in charge of this Orphanage for some time?"

"For over eight years, M'Lord."

"Then why are you so short-staffed?"

The woman looked embarrassed.

"I shouldn't have mentioned it, M'Lord, except that you finds me in such a mess. Of course, if I'd known Your Lordship and Your Ladyship were coming . . ."

"Why are you short-staffed?" Lord Colwall asked again.

"The truth is, M'Lord, there's not enough money these days. When your Lordship's grandfather endowed the Orphanage it was enough and to spare, but the pound won't buy what it used to and that's the truth."

"You mean you cannot pay for adequate help?"

"No, M'Lord. I used to have two untrained girls—some of them as young as twelve or thirteen, most of them more trouble then they are worth—but I can't even get those now. There's too many places as wants 'em."

"You say you have twenty children here?" Natalia asked.

"Yes, M'Lady. They keeps asking me to take more, but 'tis impossible. But I has to do everything, except for old Mrs. Brown who comes in the morning to help me prepare a meal."

Natalia looked at Lord Colwall.

"We cannot leave the little boy here in the condition he is in. It would be too much to ask of Mrs. Moppam."

"It's not that I'm not willing, M'Lady, but what'd I do at the moment, with an injured child on my hands? As it is, there's eight children down with Whooping Cough."

"I suppose there is the Hospital . . ." Lord Colwall began.

"Not in Hereford, M'Lord. Worcester's nearest, and that's not much of a place to send a child, from all I hear."

"Then he will come home with us."

There was a firmness in Natalia's voice which told Lord Colwall without words she was determined in this matter whatever he might say.

His lips tightened as he said:

"That perhaps will be the best solution at least for tonight."

"Thank you, M'Lord. I am very grateful, and to you, M'Lady," Mrs. Moppam said, twisting her hands agitatedly in her dirty apron.

"Good-bye, Mrs. Moppam," Natalia said with a smile. "I am sure my husband will be able to make arrangements so that you can employ more help for the other children in your care. When the Orphanage was built it was certainly intended to be a model of its kind."

She moved towards the door as she spoke.

Mrs. Moppam followed her, bobbing and curtseying apprehensively up and down as first Natalia and then Lord Colwall went towards the carriage.

The child had not moved since Natalia had left him; now she sat down on the seat and said to the footman:

"Will you lift the boy into my arms?"

The footman looked surprised, and as he was about to pick up the child, Lord Colwall said:

"Is this wise? He is very dirty and the blood will undoubtedly stain your dress."

"That is of no consequence," Natalia replied.

She took the child from the footman and made him comfortable on her lap and pulled the rug over him.

Lord Colwall said nothing and they set off towards the Castle.

As they neared the lodges, the child's eyelids fluttered and he made a feeble cry.

"It is all right," Natalia said soothingly. "You are quite safe, Timothy."

He gave a little whimper because he was obviously in pain.

Natalia eased the rug from off his leg then put her arms around him again.

"It is all right," she said rocking him backwards and forwards.

"Mama . . . Mama," he murmured, just as they reached the Castle.

The servants came hurrying out and a footman lifted Timothy from Natalia's arms.

"Take him straight up to the Nursery," she instructed.

"Very good, M'Lady."

The footman carrying Timothy carefully went ahead, and when Natalia reached the hall she saw there was a great stain of blood on the skirt of her gown.

There was also dust and mud on her bodice, where she had held the child's body close against her.

She looked at Lord Colwall for one moment as she passed him to go towards the stairs.

"Thank you for letting me bring Timothy here," she said softly so that only he could hear.

His lips were twisted for a moment in a wry smile.

"Did I have any choice in the matter?"

"Not really!" she answered, and he saw the dimple at the side of her mouth as she walked away from him.

Upstairs in the Nursery, Nanny, who had not yet gone to bed, had forgotten her arthritis and was undressing Timothy by the fire.

"What happened, M'Lady?" she asked as Natalia entered.

"We knocked him down in the road outside Hereford," Natalia explained. "He had run away from the Orphanage to look for his mother."

"Poor little mite!" Nanny ejaculated. "Children of that age do not understand."

She pulled off the Child's clothes that were little more than rags.

"You'll find a night-shirt which once belonged to His Lordship in the chest in the corner, M'Lady."

Natalia hurried to fetch it for her and then she helped Nanny wash the blood from the child's leg and hand.

Nanny bandaged him deftly, and now he was half-conscious and twisting his head from side to side, moaning and calling all the time "Mama . . . Mama."

Natalia soothed him with gentle fingers.

After he had drunk some warm milk they laid him in the small bed which still stood in the Night-Nursery beside the larger one occupied by Nurse.

It was then Nanny, looking at Natalia with a smile, asked:

"How did you persuade His Lordship to let him come here?"

"There was no alternative really," Natalia answered. "The Orphanage is desperately understaffed—only Mrs. Moppam to look after twenty children! Oh, Nanny, how could things have got into such a bad state?"

"It is always the same when there is no lady to see to things," Nanny answered. "When His Lordship's mother was alive, she knew everything that went on on the Estate."

"I learned today that she visited the cottages, but no-one had been near them since," Natalia murmured.

"Who was there to go?" Nanny enquired. "Lady Blestow only stayed here when there was entertaining to be done, and His late-Lordship was so sunk in his own sorrow he was not interested."

"I must try and help them," Natalia said almost to herself.

"That is exactly what they want!" Nanny said. "Someone like yourself to make them feel that they matter in the world. People get despondent when they are not wanted."

"That is true enough," Natalia said in a sad little voice.

Nanny glanced at her quickly and then she said:

"You go to bed, M'Lady. I'll look after Timothy and if he doesn't seem better in the morning, we'll send for the doctor. But if you ask me, there's nothing that a good rest won't cure. There's no bones broken—take my word for it!"

"I do, Nanny, and thank you!" Natalia said.

She went downstairs and to her surprise found as she reached the landing outside her bedroom that Lord Colwall was waiting for her.

"It is time you went to bed," he said. "You look tired."

"I am a little," Natalia confessed. "It was such a shock seeing the child lying there in the road and thinking we might have killed him."

"Is he all right?"

"Nanny says so."

"Then he will be!"

Natalia smiled.

"I am sure he will."

"Then go to bed and dream of pleasant things."

"I will try to," she said a little doubtfully.

Lord Colwall looked for a moment as if he wanted to say something else, and then he changed his mind and turned towards his own room.

"Good-night, Natalia."

"Good-night, My Lord."

She had a wild desire to run after him, to ask him if she could stay with him a little and they could sit by the fire talking.

Then she wondered if she was being sincere, if she really wanted to talk to him or did she in fact long for something very different!

Chapter Six

Lord Colwall arrived at the Castle in his Phaeton.

He stepped down with a look on his face which made two of the younger footmen, who were less well-trained, glance at each other in consternation.

They knew only too well that His Lordship's "black look" meant that he was in a fault-finding mood.

His Lordship handed his high beaver hat to the Butler, who then helped him off with his overcoat.

As he drew his driving-gloves from his hands he asked:

"Where is Her Ladyship?"

"I think she is upstairs, M'Lord," the Butler replied. "I will inform her that Your Lordship has returned."

"I will tell her myself!"

Lord Colwall walked up the stone staircase, conscious as he did so of a feeling of intense annoyance that Natalia was not waiting for him.

He knew he was early and he was well aware that his meeting with the High Sheriff over County matters had put him in a bad humour.

But it added to his anger that Natalia was not waiting for him on his arrival.

He made it clear to her that when they could not go riding together in the mornings, he expected to see her as soon as he returned home.

Although he would not admit it to himself, he liked to see her eyes light up at his appearance.

He opened the door of her Sitting-Room and found, as he had expected, it was empty, and frowning, he climbed the minor staircase to the next floor.

As he approached the Nursery, Lord Colwall remembered that it was many years since he had visited this part of the Castle, which he had occupied as a child.

There was, he thought, the same smell about it and as he reached the Nursery door, it was almost disappointing not to find that homemade bread was being toasted in front of the open fire, or distinguish the sickly fragrance of toffee on the air.

Instead, he heard Natalia's voice saying:

". . . And then, just as the Dragon was coming nearer and nearer, fire coming out of his nostrils, his great scaly tail waving in the air, the Princess saw someone shining and silver coming through the green trees."

" 'T'was the . . . Knight!" a little voice of one who obviously knew the story already cried excitedly.

"Yes, it was the Knight coming to rescue her!" Natalia said. "The Dragon had not seen the Knight approaching on his white charger, and now he opened his big, ugly mouth with its great big teeth to swallow the Princess up! But just as he was about to take a big bite, the Knight thrust his long lance down his throat."

"He killed him . . . He killed him!"

"Yes, he killed him, and it was a tremendous battle, but the Princess stopped screaming because she knew the Knight was going to win."

"What did the Knight do . . . then?"

The child's tone was breathless.

Natalia opened her lips to reply and a deep voice said:

"I, too, should be interested to know the end of the story."

She gave a little exclamation and saw Lord Colwall standing in the doorway

He looked as usual, extremely elegant with tight pantaloons the colour of pale champagne, and the points of his collar very high against his firm chin.

"My Lord!" Natalia exclaimed with a tone of consternation in her voice

She rose to her feet but not before Lord Colwall had

seen her arms had held Timothy closely and his small head had been resting against her breast.

"You are early!" Natalia said with a glance at the clock on the mantel-shelf.

"Only a trifle," Lord Colwall replied loftily, "but as there was no-one to welcome me downstairs, I obviously had to come in search of you."

"I am sorry you should have been troubled," Natalia said in a low voice.

There was an accusing note in his voice which she knew meant that he was incensed.

"What happened? What happened?" Timothy begged, holding on to Natalia's full skirt with his small hands.

He had recovered from his accident, but he was still very thin. His face was almost ethereal with good features and large, blue, appealing eyes, which made him exceptionally attractive.

"I see that your protégé has returned to health," Lord Colwall said.

"He is better," Natalia replied, "and the scar on his knee is healed. At the same time he is very fragile."

"He looks well enough to me," Lord Colwall said, "and as Mrs. Moppam now has assistance in the Orphanage, I have arranged for him to return there this afternoon."

"Oh, no!"

It was a cry from Natalia's heart, and as she saw the expression on Lord Colwall's face, she said quickly:

"You have provided Mrs. Moppam with girls willing to assist her?"

"I have found two," Lord Colwall answered. "Or rather my Agent has discovered them in the village. They are not more than fifteen years of age, but they are glad to have the opportunity of working. I understand they both come from large families, so they will be used to dealing with children."

"That is kind of you," Natalia approved. "I know Mrs. Moppam will be delighted."

"She is!" Lord Colwall said, "and I have increased

the annual income for the Orphanage, so that too should meet with your approval!"

There was a distinct challenge in his voice.

"I knew you would do what is right."

Lord Colwall looked away from the gratitude in Natalia's eyes.

"I am sure that, in the circumstances that now exist in the Orphanage, this child will find it impossible to run away at night, or at any other time and endanger his life."

"He is still not very . . . strong," Natalia said hesitatingly. "Could he not stay a . . . little longer?"

"No!"

The one syllable was firm.

"Why not?"

"Because it is a mistake for him to become used to a luxurious life when he will have to work his way in the world."

"That I can understand," Natalia agreed. "But at the same time he is only five years old and he misses his . . . mother."

She bent down as she spoke to lift Timothy up into her arms.

He clung to her and kissed her cheek.

"Another . . . story . . . Mama?" he pleaded.

"I see he already thinks you are his mother," Lord Colwall said. "A most undesirable illusion from the child's point of view."

"He calls every woman 'Mama,'" Natalia explained. "Nanny, Mrs. Hodges, and Ellen! In fact he is a child who needs attention."

"He is fortunate to get it," Lord Colwall said. "I myself find it in somewhat short supply."

"I am sorry," Natalia said simply. "It is nearly luncheon-time. I will wash my hands and be downstairs in a very few moments."

"And that child is to be taken back this afternoon," Lord Colwall said. "Is that understood?"

For a moment he thought Natalia might defy him. Instead she replied dully:

"I understand. I will take him . . . back."

Calling Nanny to come and look after Timothy, she ran downstairs hastily to her bed-room to find Ellen waiting for her.

As the Maid poured some warm water into a basin, Natalia said with a little sob in her voice:

"His Lordship has ordered me to take Timothy back to the Orphanage this afternoon. Oh, Ellen, he will be so unhappy again!"

"He'll miss you, M'Lady," Ellen said.

"And Nanny . . . and you," Natalia answered. "We have played with him, we have all tried to make him forget his mother, but now I feel that instead of crying for her, he will be crying for us."

"It's made all the difference to Nanny having him here, M'Lady," Ellen said. "I suppose you couldn't ask His Lordship if Timothy could stay a little longer?"

"I have asked him," Natalia answered, "and he has refused. I think His Lordship resents the time I spend in the Nursery."

As she spoke she knew that was the truth.

It was a continued irritant to Lord Colwall that she should want to be with the orphan child, when he felt she should be providing him with one of her own.

He had not said anything, but whenever she referred to the little boy, there was an expression on Lord Colwall's face which told her all too clearly what he was thinking.

"I've an idea, M'Lady," Ellen said suddenly.

"What is it?" Natalia enquired.

"My Aunt married the Blacksmith, M'Lady. His name's Turner. They lost their only child when he was nine years of age, and she's never been the same since. She can't have another and seeing how she's always been fond of children, it's been a bitter blow to them both."

Natalia's eyes were alight.

"Ellen, do you think they would adopt Timothy?"

"I'm almost sure of it, M'Lady, if you were to ask them to do so."

"I will take Timothy there this afternoon," Natalia

said. "If she refuses to take him, then I must carry him on to the Orphanage. Oh, Ellen, how clever of you to think of it!"

"It's only just come to my mind, M'Lady," Ellen said, "but it does seem a wonderful opportunity for Timothy to have a home. That's what he wants—a home! With a father and mother to care for him."

"I shall pray that Mrs. Turner will agree," Natalia said.

She went down to the Salon to find Lord Colwall looking out of the window.

It was a grey, blustery day with a promise of rain in the sky. He turned as Natalia came into the room.

With her fair hair and gown of pale daffodil yellow, she looked like a shaft of sunlight.

She smiled at him and moved towards the fireplace.

"Have you had a busy morning?" she asked.

"An extremely disagreeable one," Lord Colwall replied. "If ever there was a self-confident, obstinate man, it is the High Sheriff!"

"I hope he is not thinking the same thing about you!" she said mischievously.

"I am quite sure he is thinking a great deal more. I defeated him in every argument, and the rest of those present supported me."

"I am sure they did," Natalia answered. "After all, you are so much cleverer than the average local Big-Wig."

"How do you know that?" he asked with a faint smile.

"I know only too well how dull and pompous County Gentlemen become when they discuss local affairs," Natalia answered. "Papa used to say that nothing seemed more dreary than when he had to go to a meeting with the Gentlemen of Cumberland pontificating for the good of their kind."

Lord Colwall laughed, and Natalia realised that his bad temper was evaporating.

"I wish we could do something interesting this afternoon," he said. "Unfortunately, I have to attend yet another meeting at Hereford."

"No-one could accuse you of not taking an interest in County matters," Natalia said, "but I would like above all things to hear you speak in the House of Lords."

"On what topic?" Lord Colwall enquired.

She was about to answer him and then she realised that this was not the moment to bring up the subject of injustice to the Labourers, cruelty to the climbing boys, or the horrifying abuses of the children working in factories.

One day, she promised herself, she would discuss it with him, but not until they had a better understanding between them and he would listen to what she had to say.

Instead she tried to amuse him during luncheon, telling him stories of Cumberland, and speaking of Art, which she had learnt by now was a subject which never failed to arouse his interest.

"When we go to London," he said, "you will have a chance of seeing the pictures at Buckingham Palace. The late King, for all his faults, had a taste with which it is impossible to find fault."

"I would love to see them," Natalia said, "although I think I should be too nervous to enjoy them properly as they are in the Palace."

"You would not be nervous with the new King, nor with his wife," Lord Colwall said. "King William is a blunt, good-humoured, jovial man, very like the Cumberland Gentlemen you have described to me, and Queen Adelaide is young, shy, but very anxious to be pleasant."

"You make them sound quite a homely couple," Natalia said.

"They are!" Lord Colwall replied laconically.

He hurried away after luncheon was over and Natalia went somewhat unhappily upstairs to put on her bonnet and cloak.

As she expected, Nanny was almost in tears.

"It's been like the old days, M'Lady, and that's a fact, having a child in the Nursery," she said. "It's made me feel young again."

It was true that Nanny seemed to have grown not only younger, but a great deal stronger since Timothy had been there.

She still limped as she walked, but she managed to bustle around as she made no effort to do before, and Natalia was quite certain that her rheumatism was partly due to being inactive.

As she had promised, she had made Nanny the herbal potion according to her mother's special recipe, but she knew that the best medicine she could possibly have would be a baby to look after.

'Just another reason,' Natalia said to herself, 'why I should give His Lordship an heir.'

She knew that she wanted more than anything else to have a child and know that it would grow up as handsome and attractive as its father.

Yet her whole body shrank with the kind of sick horror when she thought that, because Lord Colwall did not love her, she might produce a deformed baby such as she had seen lying on the grave of Sarah's step-father.

She would never forget, she thought, her feelings when she had seen it!

It had been a moment when repugnance and pity mingled with a fiery anger that such a thing should have happened.

She could remember her father saying quickly and almost harshly to her mother:

"Take Natalia away. I will deal with this."

Her mother had taken her arm and drawn her towards the Church, but she knew she could never forget, and what she had seen was seared deep into her memory for all time.

"See . . . horses?" Timothy was asking with a look of excitement in his blue eyes.

"Yes, two big horses," Natalia answered.

Nanny buttoned him into a warm coat which Ellen had gone to Hereford to buy for him. There was a woollen cap to cover his fair hair and new gloves for his hands.

When he was ready, a footman carried him down

the stairs and set him beside Natalia in the comfortable brougham which she used when she went out driving alone.

There were two fine horses to draw it and two men on the box, and she thought as they moved down the drive how confortable and secure her life was compared to what the future held for the little boy at her side.

He was so frail that she felt he would never survive if, when he was old enough, he was sent to a factory or apprentised.

She had heard terrifying stories from her father of how badly apprentices could be treated. Some of them were little better then slaves, beaten and starved by their masters with no redress, unless they ran away.

Then, if they were caught, they could be brought back and beaten all over again.

'I cannot bear it for Timothy,' she thought to herself.

In the short time he had been at the Castle, she had developed a special affection for the child and she knew that he appealed to a maternal instinct which she had not known she possessed.

On her instructions the carriage stopped first at the Blacksmith's Forge.

There were a number of customers waiting outside holding their horses while there was the clang of a hammer on the anvil and the embers in the fire were glowing red.

The footman got down and opened the door.

"Your Ladyship wishes to speak with Mr. Turner?"

"No, to *Mrs.* Turner," Natalia replied.

"She lives in the house next to the Forge, M'Lady."

"Then see if she is at home," Natalia ordered.

The footman knocked at the door and when it opened, Natalia stepped down from the carriage.

She took Timothy by the hand and drew him into the Forge.

The Blacksmith looked up as she entered. He had hold of a horse's hoof and was nailing the shoe into place.

"Good afternoon, M'Lady!"

"Good afternoon, Mr. Turner!" Natalia said. "I wish to have a few words with your wife. Might this little boy, whose name is Timothy, stay and watch you?"

"He's welcome, M'Lady,"

"Stay here, Timothy," Natalia said, "and do not get in the way."

She saw that the child's face was alight with interest as he drew nearer to the Blacksmith. He loved horses and did not remember his accident, so it had left no unpleasant memories in his mind.

Natalia left the Forge and went up the short path to the house.

Mrs. Turner showed her into the parlour.

"It's a great honour, M'Lady. I'd no idea you might be calling."

"Ellen has told me about you, Mrs. Turner," Natalia answered, "and I have a very great favour to ask of you."

"A favour, M'Lady?" Mrs. Turner cried, not believing that it was possible for her to do anyone so important a favour.

Natalia sat down on a chair and explained about Timothy.

She told Mrs. Turner how lonely the child was without his mother, how he had escaped from the Orphanage to go looking for her, and how he called every woman "Mama" in a pathetic effort to find the love he had lost.

By the time she had finished speaking, there were tears in Mrs. Turner's eyes.

"I have told you all this," Natalia said in her soft voice, "because I wondered if it would be possible for you and Mr. Turner to adopt Timothy? I cannot bear to think of him at the Orphanage. He is such a gentle, quiet little boy, I feel he will not hold his own with the other children, and I cannot contemplate what will happen when he has to earn his own living."

"You mean adopt him, M'Lady?" Mrs. Turner asked.

"Is it too much to ask?" Natalia answered.

"I don't know. I've never thought of it, M'Lady. I don't know if my husband would agree. It's been a bitter blow to him that we had no more children, and a better and kinder man t'would be hard to find. 'Tis real miserable I am to feel that I've failed him."

"What I am going to suggest," Natalia said, "is that I leave Timothy here with you from tonight, and I will drive on to the Orphanage and explain to Mrs. Moppam that you are getting to know him. If Mr. Turner will not agree to keep him then perhaps you could take him back there tomorrow, or send me a message."

"We can manage that ourselves, Ma'am," Mrs. Turner said. "We has a gig."

"It does not matter which way it is done if Timothy has to go back," Natalia said, "but I am hoping and praying, Mrs. Turner, that you will find a place for him in your home."

She went back to the Forge to find Timothy entranced with the shoeing of the horses.

He had managed to get a streak of grease on his face and his hands were dirty, but he looked happy.

"Come with me, Timothy," Natalia said. "There is a lady who wants to meet you."

"Mama?" Timothy asked unexpectedly.

"Yes, Mama," Natalia said firmly.

She took the little boy into the house where Mrs. Turner was waiting.

"Why, he's beautiful!" she exclaimed.

"Mrs. Moppam will tell you all about him, should you wish to know," Natalia said.

She knelt down beside Timothy and said:

"Listen, Timothy, you are going to stay here today with Mama. Be a very good boy and I know she will tell you lots of stories. She had a little boy of her own once and he loved listening to them."

She saw the tears overflow in Mrs. Turner's eyes.

Then having kissed Timothy, she moved towards the door.

He did not seem to mind that she was leaving, as he was exploring the room. He liked a pretty shell he had found on a table near the wall.

The carriage carried Natalia on to the Orphanage. There she explained to Mrs. Moppam what had happened and met the new assistants who had been sent from the village. She noted that the place was much cleaner.

The children seemed happy. Those who had been at the orphanage for some time appeared well-fed.

At the same time, Natalia felt that Timothy wanted more than food and clothing. In contrast, the other children seemed very robust and coarser in appearance.

"What do you know about Timothy?" she asked Mrs. Moppam.

"His mother was a housemaid at a Gentleman's house," Mrs. Moppam replied. "She got into trouble and was turned out without a reference. She managed to keep herself and the child alive by hard work but gradually her strength gave out, I understand her lungs were affected.

"Who was the father?" Natalia asked.

"She'd never say, M'Lady, but I happens to know the house where she was employed and the son is a pleasant-spoken, handsome young gentleman."

She paused:

"The woman who brought Timothy here was with his mother when she died. She had told her that she had only ever loved one man in her life, and that he had loved her.

" 'There was never any hope for us,' she said, 'but we loved each other.' "

"So Timothy was a love-child!" Natalia exclaimed.

It was, she thought, something she had known from the moment she had seen him. Only a child that had been born in love could have looked like Timothy.

She drove back to the Castle feeling she was leaving something of herself behind her, something she should have cherished and held on to.

Then she thought it was because she missed the affection she could expend on Timothy.

She longed to put her arms around Lord Colwall and tell him she not only loved him as a man, but as someone she could comfort and look after.

She found herself continually thinking of how much he must have suffered when he learnt of his first wife's deception and immorality. He was decent, upright, and proud and the shock must have been intolerable.

He was like a child that had been hurt. That was why she longed to give him a love he had never known.

Always he had been alone. Always he had had to control his feelings and perhaps when he was small like Timothy, he had called for a mother who was dead.

'I love him!' Natalia said to herself, 'but until he loves me I cannot give him what I know he needs.'

Lord Colwall had not yet returned when she went up to dress for dinner.

She chose one of the most attractive of her gowns, knowing that the pale blue satin and rosebud tulle made a perfect foil for her fair hair and white skin.

She wore a necklace of turquoises and diamonds and there was a bracelet and ring to match, so that when she went downstairs she felt that Lord Colwall would be pleased with her appearance.

She had heard him return while she was still dressing but the Salon was empty when she entered it.

As she walked towards the fire she saw that lying on the table were the day's newspapers.

She picked up the *Morning Post* and had been reading it for some minutes when Lord Colwall came into the room.

She put the newspaper down hastily.

"Is there any interesting news?" he asked. "I have not had time to read the papers today."

Natalia did not answer him for a moment fearing that what she had been reading might annoy him.

He was obviously waiting for an answer, and after a moment she said a little hesitatingly:

"I was reading that the Duke of Buckinghamshire has said that fifteen hundred rioters in Hampshire have threatened to attack any farmhouse where there are threshing-machines."

"I believe there are a few magistrates who are cowed into submitting to mob violence." Lord Colwall said sharply. "Sir Robert Peel is determined that a firm hand must be applied from the very onset."

"But the labourers are obeying this Captain Swing. It says that wherever he appears they listen to him bareheaded."

"If he comes here," Lord Colwall replied, "we will be ready for him. I have been discussing the matter this afternoon, and here we are prepared to quell the first sign of rebellion the moment it appears."

Natalia did not reply.

She longed to plead with Lord Colwall once again to dispense with the threshing-machine and not to incite the labourers to violence but she was certain he would not listen to her.

"The sentences are to be heavier than ever," Lord Colwall went on. "Any man who starts a fire or threatens a farmer will, in future, be transported for life!"

"They are only asking for . . . justice," Natalia faltered.

"That is not the way to get it."

Dinner was announced before he could say any more and because Natalia realised that argument would achieve nothing, she deliberately spoke of other things.

"I have something to show you after dinner," Lord Colwall said, "which I think will interest you."

"What is it?" Natalia enquired with some curiosity.

"I saw a picture this afternoon which I bought."

"A picture?" she exclaimed.

"It belonged to a gentleman who has lost a great deal of money at gaming," Lord Colwall explained. "He asked me if I would like to purchase two of his horses, but they were not up to my standard and I refused them. However when I was leaving his house I saw a picture which took my fancy."

"I am looking forward to seeing it," Natalia replied. "Who is it by?"

"Sir Joshua Reynolds," Lord Colwall announced. "It's owner was asking a somewhat fancy price for it —over two hundred pounds—but I thought it was worth it."

When dinner was over he took Natalia into the Library and showed her the picture.

It was of a very beautiful woman turning sideways,

her hand outstretched, towards an urn on which was perched a small bird.

It had been painted exquisitely and Natalia gave a little cry of delight as soon as she saw it.

"It is lovely!" she exclaimed. "I am so glad that you bought it. The Lady has such grace!"

"I think that is why she reminded me of you," Lord Colwall said.

"Of me?"

She was surprised and the colour rose to her cheeks.

"I am very flattered that you should think me graceful," she said. "I have always thought that I was rather jiggety!"

"What do you mean by that?" he asked.

"Rather like a little bird which hops from twig to twig! I have always longed to fly slowly with great flapping wings as the larger birds do. That is what I think of as grace."

Lord Colwall put his arm on the mantel-shelf and looked down at her pointed face upturned to his.

"You are not like a bird," he said slowly, "You remind me of a small fawn. You have that same look in your large eyes that a fawn has! And you know how they scamper swiftly away, moving with a rhythmic grace which is almost indescribable."

"I am very pleased to be a fawn!"

She smiled at him, and then he said almost harshly:

"Of course, as an experienced hunter, I should not let the fawn get away."

"That sounds very primitive."

"Men are primitive!" Lord Colwall argued. "Have you not realised that by now? If I had behaved according to pattern, I should have dragged you away by force into my cave, just as my earliest ancestor would have done."

"Your earliest ancestor would have chosen his woman from a crowd of eligible females," Natalia replied. "He undoubtedly would have had to fight for her, and only when he had proved himself would he have been entitled to possess her."

Lord Colwall seated himself near the fire in the high-backed chair which he usually occupied.

"The trouble with you, Natalia," he said, "is you think too much! You use your brain, and brain in a woman is a nuisance and a hindrance to her femininity."

"I am sure you would much rather I was a simpering Miss who would agree with everything you said!" Natalia retorted. "But would you not find it rather dull?"

"I like women to comply with my wishes and be prepared to obey my commands."

Natalia gave him a little smile.

"I very much doubt it," she said. "You have too many brains of your own! Can you imagine anything worse than having to live permanently with someone who mouthed platitudes, never read a book, had no knowledge of Art, and would anticipate everything you wanted before you had time to formulate your needs to yourself?"

"That is exactly what I had hoped to find in my wife," Lord Colwall affirmed.

"If I believed you, I suppose that I should be humiliated into thinking how far I had fallen short of your ideal," Natalia replied. "But somehow I think that such an idea has no real substance."

She laughed.

"You wanted a doll, one of those wooden dolls I owned as a child, with a perpetual smile on its face! When you remembered to play with it, it would be there, and when you did not want it you would throw it in a corner and forget all about it!"

"Are you trying to tell me that it would be difficult to forget you?" Lord Colwall asked.

Natalia did not answer.

Herald had crept close to her as he always did, and she patted and caressed the great mastiff as he edged himself nearer and nearer in his delight at her touch.

"Did you take the child back?" Lord Colwall asked unexpectedly.

Natalia had a feeling he had been wanting all the evening to ask her this question and had been unable to bring himself to do so.

"Ellen had the wonderful idea," Natalia answered, "that her Aunt who is married to the Blacksmith might like to adopt Timothy. I have left him there for to-night, and if the Turners decide not to keep him, we can send him back to the Orphanage either tomorrow or the next day."

"You are determined he shall not go back," Lord Colwall said.

"He is such a sensitive little boy," Natalia explained, "not like the other children."

"Why should you think that?" Lord Colwall enquired.

Natalia did not answer and after a moment he said again:

"Tell me, Natalia, why should you think Timothy different from the other children?"

"There is . . . something about him," she faltered. "But perhaps they are all the . . . same, and it is . . . just that I have come to . . . know Timothy."

"What else is he?" Lord Colwall asked.

Natalia looked up at him.

"I see you . . . know already . . . My Lord, that Timothy is a . . . love-child."

"That is the answer," Lord Colwall said sharply. "That is why I wanted him out of the house. He was merely pandering to this ridiculous obstinacy of yours."

He paused and then continued:

"Now that you are no longer upset by what you overheard by mistake, surely you realise that your ideas are exaggerated. Let us live a normal married life, Natalia, and then I can prove to you that we can find a great deal of satisfaction in each other, and perhaps a great deal of pleasure."

Natalia did not answer and he went on:

"It is not a bad foundation, as anyone would tell you, on which to base a successful marriage."

There was a note in his voice which Natalia found hard to resist.

She wanted desperately to put out her hand towards him, to tell him that she would do what he wished.

She thought how easy it would be to let him kiss her, to pretend to herself that he loved her enough for them to find some sort of happiness, even if it was not the one she had envisaged for so long.

Perhaps if she succumbed to his pleadings, if she did as he wanted, he would in time love her as she wished to be loved.

He would grow to rely on her, and she was sure that if she gave him the son he wanted, then he would be, if nothing else, extremely grateful.

But was that enough?

Would their children be strong and handsome? Beautiful of face and mind? Or would they reflect that ugliness, even perhaps that horror, that she was unable to escape?

Whatever she might say with her lips, she knew she would be unable to forget Sarah's baby.

Moreover, it was impossible not to remember the coldness in Lord Colwall's voice when he had spoken with Sir James after the wedding.

How, she asked herself, could she speak to him in moments of intimacy, of love, when he had said so scathingly:

"There is no place for that nauseating, over-exaggerated emotion in my life."

'Why can I not make him love me?' Natalia asked, in her heart.

She felt suddenly very alone, very helpless!

Without really realising what she was doing, she put her cheek down against Herald's head and held him even closer against her.

Lord Colwall was watching the picture she made in her blue gown, the diamonds glittering at her throat and her bare arms around the huge animal.

There was something weak and defenceless in her attitude, and yet Lord Colwall knew her will was strong enough to keep her emotions under control, to resist the desires and needs of her own heart.

Natalia had not answered his question and he knew it was because she could not find words.

Then suddenly, as if something snapped within him, he said furiously:

"Leave that damned dog alone! Do you not think I am aware of what you are trying to do? You are trying to beguile me into falling in love with you. You are deliberately attempting to attack me, but I can assure you I am well aware of your wiles and the way your mind is working!"

Natalia raised her head at the anger in his voice and stared at him, her eyes wide.

"You are like all women," he raged. "Because you cannot get your own way, you are tempting me. But I promise you that if you go on like this you will be sorry!"

Natalia was very still and now he rose to his feet, his eyes blazing with a fire from which she shrank visibly.

"You will drive me too far! I am endeavouring to behave like a gentleman and not to force myself upon you because you are young and because you are apparently sincere in this nonsensical, hysterical notion!"

He struck the mantel-piece with his clenched fist.

"But mark my words, Natalia, I will not be responsible for my actions if you continue to behave as you are behaving now."

"What . . . have I . . . done?" Natalia murmured, finding it hard to speak because Lord Colwall's anger had made her heart thump furiously in her breast.

"It is not only what you have done," he said angrily, "it is how you look, what you say! It is everything about you! For God's sake, give me a little peace, or else I swear to you I shall force you into behaving as my wife!"

He seemed almost to spit the last words at her.

Then as she still sat looking up at him in bewilderment, one arm still around Herald, her eyes large and frightened in her pale face, Lord Colwall went from the room.

He slammed the door loudly behind him.

Chapter Seven

Natalia was not asleep when Ellen called her the following morning. In fact she had been awake practically the whole night.

After Lord Colwall had left her alone in the Library she had gone very slowly upstairs to her room, and when her Maids had left her alone she had lain in the great four-poster feeling as if the whole future was dark.

For the first time since she had come to the Castle, she experienced a sense of hopelessness and depression which hung over her like a black cloud.

Even when she had first learnt that Lord Colwall did not love her, it was not the same feeling that she had now, of a despair for which she could find no relief.

All night long she had been haunted by the roughness in his voice and the violence with which he had spoken.

All night long she could see his eyes looking at her with an expression which she felt must be one of hatred.

'What am I to do?' she asked the darkness and found no answer.

She wanted above anything else to run to her mother, to seek the comfort and the understanding that Lady Margaret had always been able to give her.

Then she told herself it would be too humiliating to crawl home and confess that her marriage was a failure when she had been so confident, so absolutely sure it would be a success.

'What can I do? What can I do?' she asked again and again.

She felt she was in truth incarcerated in one of the dungeons below the Castle without light and without any hope of escape.

"It's a nice morning, M'Lady," Ellen said as she drew back the curtains. "There was a hard frost in the night but the sun's a-coming out."

Natalia did not reply and after a moment Ellen asked as she busied herself around the room:

"Will you be riding with His Lordship this morning?"

"No," Natalia replied, "I have a headache."

"Then I'll bring your breakfast to you, M'Lady."

Another housemaid came in to light the fire, and when it was burning brightly two Maids carried in the large bath-tub in which Natalia bathed.

They set it down in front of the fire so that it was ready for her when she wished to rise.

Breakfast, elegantly served on silver crested dishes with plates of Sèvres china, was as usual delicious, but Natalia felt that anything she ate would choke her!

She drank a little tea and nibbled one or two of the large purple grapes which came from the greenhouses.

When Ellen took away her tray she exclaimed reproachfully:

"You've eaten nothing, M'Lady. Do you think you've caught a chill?"

"No, I am all right," Natalia answered.

She rose from her bed and slipping her arms through her heavy silk wrapper walked to the window to look out.

It seemed almost incongruous that the sun should be shining so brightly through the morning mists, turning the frost on the trees and shrubs into a sparkling enchantment.

How could everything be so beautiful when she herself was so low and depressed?

Then in the Park beyond the garden she saw a figure on horseback, and felt her heart quicken and come alive.

It was impossible not to admire the way Lord Colwall rode, the manner in which he sat a horse as if he was part of the animal.

In fact, only to see him was to love him.

Even at this distance, Natalia thought, she could see how handsome he was, could admire the manner in which he wore his high-crowned hat on the side of his head, and the slimness of his legs in his shining boots.

She felt as if her love welled up inside her, dispersing the darkness.

'I love him,' she murmured beneath her breath, and in that moment she knew what she must do.

'I have been absurd!' she told herself. 'Perhaps it was the shock of hearing he did not love me that made me behave as I did. If we are together, if I become his wife as he wants me to do, then I am sure that in time my love will evoke an answering response within him.'

She had forgotten, she now thought, in her obsession over Sarah's baby, that it had been born without any love, either from Sarah or from its father.

In her case it would be very different, because she loved Lord Colwall to distraction.

'I love him so much that I would die for him,' she thought. 'So why do I not live to please him?'

Quite suddenly the way seemed clear. Her love would be enough for both of them as far as their child was concerned.

If it was a son he would be strong and handsome, fine and noble like his father; and if it was a girl, there was plenty of time for them to have a son later, perhaps half a dozen!

'How stupid I have been! How foolish to have wasted so much time!' Natalia berated herself.

She moved across the room to tug at the bell-pull.

She wanted to be with Lord Colwall now—at once —to tell him that for the future everything would be different, that there would be no more reason for him to be angry with her—no reason to be incensed by her childish attitude.

'I have not been thinking straight,' Natalia excused herself.

But she knew that her father would be ashamed at her failure to think out everything carefully before she acted.

'If only I had not overheard that conversation,' she murmured. 'My wedding-day would have been different.'

It was too late now for regrets.

All she could do now would be to see that in the future Lord Colwall was happy as she wanted him to be.

'We have so many things in common,' she thought. 'We have so much to talk about, to discuss. When I am close to him, he will understand how deeply I feel about injustice and cruelty.'

She felt herself quiver with excitement at the thought of being in his arms, and when Ellen came into the room she said with a lilt in her voice:

"I want to get up, Ellen. Bring me my riding-habit."

"You're going riding, M'Lady?"

"Yes, order a horse. I will catch up with His Lordship. I know where he has gone."

She knew that Lord Colwall was trying out a new stallion which he had bought recently and she had already learnt that the best place to school an animal was where, some distance from the Castle, there was almost the equivalent of a race-course.

The ground was flat with no dangerous rabbit-holes in it, and the hedges had each been cut to a perfect height for a jump.

Natalia had already raced Lord Colwall on what was known as "The Course" on several occasions.

'That is where he will be now,' she thought to herself as she dressed. 'I will challenge him as I have done before.'

There was a sparkle in her eyes, and when she turned to look at her reflection in the mirror she saw that she was looking extremely pretty.

Ellen had produced a new riding-habit for her which she had not worn before. Of emerald-green velvet, it was warmer than the one she usually wore and was most becoming to her fair hair and white skin.

"Do you think you will be warm enough, M'Lady?" Ellen asked.

"I am sure I shall," Natalia replied.

But Ellen insisted on bringing her a satin scarf shaped almost like a cravat. She put it round her neck and tucked it into the front of her riding-coat.

"It is always hot when one is riding," Natalia smiled.

As she spoke she knew that she was glowing with the anticipation of seeing Lord Colwall and telling him that the gulf which had lain between them no longer existed.

She hurried down the stone stairs to find her horse was waiting for her at the door. It was the roan she had ridden before, and he responded immediately to her eagerness to be on her way.

"Is Your Ladyship sure you wouldn't like me to accompany you?" the groom asked.

Natalia shook her head.

"I am joining His Lordship."

Then she was trotting down the drive, eager to reach the Park where she could give her horse his head.

She galloped for some way and then as she turned from the Park onto a stubble field beyond, Natalia saw at the far end of it a crowd of men congregated around one of the big barns.

There were half-a-dozen of these built around a stockade where some of the cattle were kept in the winter.

Natalia was just going to hurry on when she saw a riderless horse and thought that it might be Lord Colwall's.

Accordingly, she turned her horse's head and as she drew nearer to the barn realised that the men whom she had seen had gone inside.

The horse, however, was left tethered to a post.

She looked at it as she approached and felt that it was not a fine enough animal to belong to His Lordship, and yet she was not quite sure.

She had not seen the new stallion of which he had spoken and she could not remember what colour he had said it was.

She rode up to the barn. The big doors were open and she could see a number of men moving about inside talking noisily.

Then she heard the sound of hammering and wondered what they could be about.

"Is His Lordship there?" she shouted but her voice seemed lost in the general confusion.

Because she felt that he must be there and at the same time, she was curious, she dismounted. Holding her horse by its bridle, she entered the barn.

For a moment, stepping from the sunlight into the darkness, it was difficult for her to see anything and then she realised there was a sudden silence.

All the men who had been talking so loudly had ceased speaking and had turned their faces towards her.

"Is His Lordship . . ." she began.

Then she saw that behind the men stood a huge piece of machinery.

Without asking she knew what it was! A threshing-machine! The monster of which she had read so much and which had aroused such violent feelings all over the country.

She stared at it and saw that a number of men were already standing on it and holding large hammers in their hands.

"What are you doing?" she asked and knew the answer even before she asked the question.

"May I enquire who this Lady is?" a cultured voice asked.

Natalia turned her head from the contemplation of the machine to see a man moving towards her among the crowd of labourers.

He was about medium height and fashionably dressed, but there was something pretentious and rather garish about him which told her he was in fact no aristocrat.

"This be Her Ladyship, Captain," one of the labourers said in a low voice.

"Indeed! Then you are Lady Colwall?"

"Yes, I am," Natalia answered, "and may I enquire your name?"

"I have many names," the man replied with an unpleasant twist to his thick lips.

He was in fact good-looking in a somewhat vulgar manner and he had an air about him of such self-assurance that it implied a vast self-conceit.

"Many names?" Natalia repeated in perplexity.

Then she realised that one of the men had called him "Captain."

"You are . . . Captain Swing?" she said accusingly.

He bowed to her ironically.

"The evil genius who is behind the riots which are taking place in so many Counties!" Natalia went on.

"Your Ladyship flatters me!"

"I do not intend to do so," she replied fiercely. "You have no right to come here and incite our men to violence."

She saw the sneer on his lips and continued:

"You know as well as I do that if they break up this machine, they will be imprisoned and undoubtedly transported. How can you inflict such suffering upon them?"

"Us be only a-trying t'get our rights, M'Lady," one of the men muttered.

Natalia looked at their honest, rather stupid faces.

She knew several of the men by sight, and she was quite sure that they would none of them ever have taken such action if they had not been skilfully led into rebellion by this notorious Captain Swing.

"Listen to me," she insisted. "You know as well as I do that His Lordship will not tolerate the destruction of his property, or insurrection amongst his own people. Do not listen to what this man says—this outsider who has caused so much trouble in so many other Counties and achieved nothing."

"He says that a lot o'landowners have put up th' wages," one of the men remarked.

"That is true, Lady Colwall," Captain Swing interposed. "On a great number of farms we have been most successful."

"Not for the men who have actually taken the initiative!" Natalia retorted. "They are languishing in prison awaiting trial and you know the kind of sentence they will receive."

She turned again to the men.

"Have you thought if you are taken to prison how your wives and families will suffer? Perhaps His Lordship will not allow them to remain in his cottages."

She paused and added pleadingly:

"Let me speak to him on your behalf. Do not do anything so foolish as to destroy this machine or fire the ricks until you have spoken to His Lordship man to man about your problems."

"Proud words!" Captain Swing sneered. "But do you imagine that His Lordship will listen? The first man who opposes a landowner is clapped into prison before he can even open his mouth."

He looked around at the listening men.

"Only if we all act together, if we show these blood-sucking employers that we mean business, will anything ever get done!"

"You're right, Captain! That be true enough," a man shouted.

"It is not true!" Natalia cried angrily. "His Lordship has no idea that you are discontented. Your wage is above the average, but I agree it is not enough. I have already spoken to him, asking that you should receive more, and that extra money should be given for every child."

"If you've spoken to M'Master, what did he reply?" a voice asked from the back of the crowd.

"What I am suggesting," Natalia said, ignoring the question, "is that you speak with His Lordship before you do anything so rash as to render yourselves liable for transportation or even worse."

Captain Swing laughed.

"Can't you see she's trying to frighten you?" he asked the labourers. "It's the usual threatening talk. 'Lay one finger on my property, and you'll swing from the gallows'—you've heard it all before and in the meantime, men and women starve!"

"You certainly do not look as if you yourself are starving, Captain!" Natalia said sharply.

"You must not always judge by appearances, M'Lady," he replied suavely. "And now perhaps you should run along and leave us to get on with our business, which I assure you, is of National importance!"

"It is a business that might end up on the gallows," Natalia warned. "These men are my husband's employees and his responsibility. I will not allow you to encourage them to commit crimes that can only end in disaster."

"And how will you prevent me?" Captain Swing asked.

He asked the question with an amused note in his voice, and then, as he looked at her, his eyes narrowed.

"I have an idea," he said, "which I am sure will meet with Your Ladyship's approval."

"What is it?" Natalia asked, a little apprehensively.

For the first time since she had come into the barn, she felt afraid.

She knew now there was something evil about Captain Swing and had the idea too that he was slightly unbalanced.

She could understand how, because he was smart and glib and gave the appearance of being a gentleman, he could easily sway the poor, stupid labourers. They had never yet had anyone to speak on their behalf and were therefore easily inflamed by his recitation of their ills.

"I have thought of a better way to get what we want on this Estate," Captain Swing said slowly.

"What be that, Captain?" one of the men asked.

"Instead of breaking up His Lordship's machine, or even firing his ricks, we will take possession of something which I imagine is even more valuable to him."

"And what might that be?" a man enquired.

"We'll take a hostage," Captain Swing replied, "and who better than Her Ladyship?"

He moved towards Natalia as he spoke and instinctively she took a step backwards. A man standing near her took hold of her horse's bridle.

"Do not dare touch me!" she cried. "If any harm comes to me, His Lordship will bring Troops against you all."

Captain Swing took her arm and when she tried to shake herself free she found he did not release her.

She did not know what he was going to do and she felt a definite tremor of fear.

"Do not listen to him," she begged the men. "Can you not understand that when he has incited you to do something that is illegal, he will disappear. He has not been caught in Kent or Sussex, Surrey or Gloucestershire, but the labourers there paid the penalty for their crimes. Do not heed anything that he may say!"

"Fine words, M'Lady!" Captain Swing remarked. "But I have the feeling that, because you are far from unattractive, His Lordship will be extremely anxious to have you back, and our terms will be quite simple."

"Where're ye a-going t'put her, Captain?" a man asked.

"That's what you are going to tell me," Captain Swing replied. "It has to be somewhere where His Lordship'll not find her, and that rules out any buildings on the farm and your cottages."

"Do you really think," Natalia asked furiously, "that His Lordship will submit to blackmail?"

"He won't like to think of you hungry, cold and very uncomfortable," Captain Swing replied. "And doubtless he will be anxious for the return of his pretty Bride, not having been married long enough to have tired of you—as all men tire in time."

"Oi've thought of a place, Captain," one of the young labourers said.

"And where might that be?" the Captain asked.

"Th' ol' Mill."

There was a murmur from the others as if they approved the idea.

"No-un has used it for years. 'Tis derelict, and Oi

doubt if the Master be aware it be still there. 'Tis supposed t'be haunted."

"The very place," the Captain smiled. "Are you afraid of ghosts, My Lady?"

"I am afraid of nothing! Not even of you!" Natalia replied. "But I am genuinely distressed that these foolish men should listen to you. You are evil, and they do not realise it."

"Now come along, my lads. There's no time to stand here talking," the Captain said. "What we want is action! How far is this place?"

"Less than half a mile, Captain, and if us goes along th'bank o' th'stream, no-un'll see us."

"A good idea!" Captain Swing approved. "Two of you come with me and see that our prisoner does not escape. The rest of you go back to work!"

"What about th' horse?" asked the man who was holding it.

"Keep it out of sight," the Captain commanded. "We'll return it later to the stables with a note for His Lordship, setting out our terms."

"Very good, Captain."

They hurried to obey his orders with a quickness which showed Natalia how much they stood in awe of him.

It was hopeless, she thought, to try to persuade them any further. They would listen only to him. He was their champion, their leader, and they were ready to obey him slavishly.

The boy who had thought of the derelict Mill went ahead and Captain Swing, still holding Natalia by the arm, followed while two others walked behind.

They kept in the shade of the willows bordering a small stream, which ran beside the farm and twisted its way through open fields.

The long grass beneath the willows was white with frost and soon the velvet skirt of Natalia's riding-habit was wet and she could feel the damp seeping through the short ankle-length boots she was wearing.

She was certain too that her white, lace-edged petti-

coat would soon also be soaked. But this was not the
moment to worry over minor details.

What really perturbed her was how soon Lord Colwall would learn that she had been taken hostage, and
what action he would take.

After they had been walking a little while, Captain
Swing released her arm.

"I'm suggesting it would not be sensible to try to
escape. I'm quite fleet of foot and I doubt if you
could out-run any of us."

"I shall not do anything so foolish," Natalia answered proudly. "I shall merely wait for His Lordship
to rescue me, which he will undoubtedly do. Then
those poor idiots you have persuaded into agreeing to your nefarious schemes will be punished."

"Proud words, M'Lady!" Captain Swing said with a
grin, "but before your husband receives you back into
his manly arms, he'll agree to our terms—otherwise
he'll not learn where to find you."

"Someone will undoubtedly tell him." Natalia said.

"You are being over-optimistic," Captain Swing replied. "I assure you that these men are loyal to me and
to themselves. They know how much depends on their
solidarity—how much they stand to gain, and how little
to lose."

"Only their freedom!" Natalia snapped.

"Freedom to starve because a threshing-machine is
taking away their livelihood?" Captain Swing asked.

Because it was difficult not to agree with him, Natalia pressed her lips together and made no reply.

They walked on in silence until a turn of the stream
brought them in sight of the old Mill.

"It certainly looks dilapidated!" Captain Swing remarked.

Natalia's heart sank as she realised she had never
seen it before and there was every likelihood that His
Lordship had forgotten its existence.

The trees had grown up densely all round the building so that from a distance, she thought, it would be
indiscernible.

Shrubs stood thick around the pool and the great wheel was rusted.

The boy walking ahead of them pulled open the door which was practically off its hinges.

"Th' room be at th'top," he said, pointing his finger. " 'Tis where they used to keep th'grain."

Natalia looked apprehensively at the rickety stairway; one rail had broken away and some of the slats were missing.

"Is it safe?" the Captain asked the boy.

He was obviously referring to the stairway.

"Safe enough," the boy replied. "Oi often went oop there when Oi was a kid."

"Very well," the Captain said. "You go first and Her Ladyship will follow you."

"Th' only thing ye didna' want t'do is t'fall into th'pool. There be a current in it that'll suck ye down. Nothing that goes in ever comes oop again!"

"Then that is something we must all avoid. Come along, My Lady!"

Reluctantly, though there was nothing else she could do, Natalia climbed the rickety stairway.

The boy who had gone ahead opened the door at the top and she saw a small, square room where the grain had been kept.

It was completely empty and the one window had been boarded up roughly so that only a few chinks of light came through it. But it was enough to show her that the room, unlike the approach to it, was strong and secure.

Captain Swing looked around him with satisfaction.

"I regret," he said, "that we cannot provide Your Ladyship with any furniture, not even the pallet to which prisoners are usually entitled! Let us hope that you will not have to linger here for long."

Natalia heard the boy rattling down the stairs again.

She was alone with Captain Swing and she turned to look at him, realising that in the dim light which came through the boarded-up window he looked even more evil and unpleasant.

"Let me beg of you, Captain," she pleaded, "to reconsider your actions. You must know what terrible retribution will be brought upon the men who work here. I agree with you that the wages are low, but this is not the way to improve their lot—not when dealing with a man like my husband!"

"I think we shall find that His Lordship will be amenable," Captain Swing replied with a leer. "You're a very pretty young woman, Lady Colwall, and he will undoubtedly find his bed a lonely place without you."

The impertinence of his words made Natalia draw herself up proudly.

"Then there is nothing more to be said, Captain Swing," she said coldly. "My husband, I am sure, will deal with the matter most effectively. I only hope you will be there when the moment comes!"

"Your courage does you credit."

The Captain bowed ironically, then went out through the door which led to the stairway, and Natalia heard a heavy bolt shoot into place.

She sat still listening to the sound of his footsteps going cautiously down the stairway.

There was a murmur of voices below as he gave the men some orders, and after a moment or two there was silence.

She walked across the room to pull at some of the boards which covered the window, but found it impossible to move them.

She then tried the door knowing even as she did so it was hopeless.

There only remained the shaft down to the floor below, but this too was boarded up. It was in fact, she had to admit, a very effective prison.

She would not suffocate as there was plenty of fresh air coming through the gaps in the boards.

She knew, however, that if she were to be cooped up here until late in the day, she would become very cold.

She began to walk up and down, realising that while she was warm now from the walk, she would need to exercise herself continuously when the sun began to set in the afternoon.

She told herself that she must be rescued before then, but she felt in fact far from sure of it.

She reckoned that the time was now about half past ten o'clock in the morning. It was doubtful if His Lordship would return to the Castle before noon.

Presumably Captain Swing's letter informing him that she had been taken as a hostage would be waiting for him.

She hardly dared to contemplate how angry Lord Colwall would be, and what was more, she told herself with a little sigh, he was certain to think it was her own fault!

Perhaps it had been stupid of her to have gone to the barn, but how could she have known that the horse was not his?

It was easy now to regret that she had not taken a groom with her, but she had been so sure that she had only to catch up with His Lordship and they would ride together for the rest of the morning, as they had done so often before.

She sat down on the floor and tried to think, but all she could remember was the sneer on Captain Swing's face, his mockery of her efforts to persuade the men to do nothing rash, the confidence he showed in his ability to cause trouble.

'He has been so clever,' she told herself. 'Everywhere he has been, he has incited the labourers to intimidate their employers by firing the ricks and breaking up the threshing-machines. Then he slips away and is never caught.'

There was no doubt in her mind that the labourers had been unjustly treated, but at the same time this type of revolution had no chance of success.

There might be a few farmers who would give in to threats, but the majority of landowners would fight back with the help of the Military and the magistrates. How then could a few uneducated labourers stand up against them?

Yet she could not help feeling that in a way Lord Colwall had brought this upon himself.

He could not have chosen a worse moment of all the times of the year to install a threshing-machine.

There was no doubt that the Government was taking the riots in Kent, Sussex and the other Southern Counties very seriously, and the fact that the unrest was spreading to other places would only increase their resolution to show no mercy to the rioters.

Natalia remembered how a man called Legge had been sentenced to death and she thought despairingly that Lord Colwall himself would show no mercy to any men who rioted on his Estate.

'I must escape! I must!' she said to herself.

She rose to pull again at the pieces of wood which boarded up the window, only to find as she had before that to move then was quite beyond her strength.

They were each held in place by several long nails.

She wondered if there would be any point in crying for help, but knew it was hopeless. She managed to peer through a slit in the boards and she could see fields stretching away into the distance but not a soul in sight.

At this time of the year there was little activity on the land and, even if there were any labourers within hearing, she felt quite certain that following Captain Swing's instructions they would make no attempt to rescue her.

There was nothing she could do but sit down and wait for His Lordship to give in to Captain Swing's demands, and when he had vanished, to wreak revenge upon the men who must remain on the Estate.

'I must pray,' Natalia told herself.

She sat down again, making herself as comfortable as possible in a corner of the room.

She prayed for a little while, then found herself thinking of her Knight and how, when she had imagined a similar situation, he had always managed to rescue her in the face of impossible odds.

'Captain Swing is indeed a powerful Dragon,' she thought.

She remembered how she had held Timothy close

in her arms and how much he had enjoyed the story of the Knight in shining armour who had attacked the frightening Dragon.

She had hoped this afternoon to learn that the Blacksmith and his wife would adopt Timothy.

At the thought of the little boy, she began to imagine the stories that she would tell her own children when she had them.

'How they would love the Castle,' she thought. 'What child's imagination would not be fired by the deeds of valour which had won the treasures hanging on the walls, performed by men who had worn the armour which lined the passages and corridors.'

To think of her children was inevitably to think of Lord Colwall. How handsome, how clever, he was!

'When I see His Lordship again,' Natalia promised herself, 'I will tell him why I was hurrying to find him this morning.'

She felt herself quiver with the excitement she had known when she had set out from the Castle.

When he understood why she had been trying to find him, she knew there would be a sudden light in his eyes, and the scowl would lift from his forehead.

He would kiss her, as she had always longed for him to do!

She wanted more than she could express in words the feel of his lips and the touch of his hands! She knew it would be like Heaven to be in his arms.

"I love him! I love him!"

She said the words aloud and heard them echo round the small room.

"I love him!"

There was almost a resonance in it as her voice struck the walls.

One day he would love her, one day she would make him happy and he would be able to forget Lady Claris and how she had made him suffer.

The hours seemed to drag on slowly. By the time it was afternoon, Natalia began to feel hungry.

She wished now she had eaten her breakfast, and she thought regretfully of the succulent dishes she had waved away because she had been feeling so depressed.

An hour later she knew the sun had gone and what light there was in the small room was fading rapidly.

Now the air was getting icy cold and Natalia walked up and down as briskly as she could—ten steps one way and ten steps back. But she could already feel the chill penetrate through her velvet jacket.

She was thankful now that Ellen had insisted on her taking the green scarf. She had pulled off her hat so that she could sit more comfortably in the corner, and she wondered if the gauze veil which encircled the high crown would bring her any warmth—but decided it was unlikely.

Backwards and forwards! Up and down!

She knew it would be stupid to stop, but after an hour she began to feel tired—tired of the confining space—tired of the smell of age, dust and mildew!

And tired of being alone, of wondering why she had not been rescued.

'Supposing,' she thought to herself in some consternation, 'His Lordship decides to defy the rioters? Supposing he refuses to give in to their requests?'

The idea had not occurred to her before. She had imagined that, incensed though he would be, Lord Colwall would not leave her unprotected in Captain Swing's hands.

She was suddenly still in apprehension.

Supposing, because she meant so little to him, he considered it more important to stick to his principles than to rescue her?

If he sent for the Military, it was unlikely they could arrive before late tomorrow, perhaps even the next day!

She was rather vague as to where soldiers were likely to be stationed in that part of the country, but she had a vague idea that she had heard someone say there were barracks at Worcester.

If Lord Colwall had received the letter at luncheon time, how long would it take a groom to ride to Worcester and the men to march back?

Natalia found it difficult to think clearly. So many

new possibilities appeared to present themselves. So many problems she had not visualized before.

"Oh, come for me! Come for me," she found herself whispering.

She felt as if her need for Lord Colwall must wing its way across the fields and tell him how greatly she longed for him.

She was afraid now. Afraid he did not care enough to save her, and was indifferent to her suffering because she had angered him last night. Also he might well not realise the urgency of coming to her rescue.

Supposing she was left here indefinitely?

Then Natalia told herself sharply she was letting her imagination run away with her, as had happened so often before.

It was no use thinking such things. He would come— of course he would come!

He might be angered with her, but he would wish to protect his wife from unpleasantness.

"Come for me! I want you, I want you!" She found herself murmuring the words aloud and realised as she spoke that her lips were very cold.

'I must walk up and down again,' she told herself, and then felt it was almost too much trouble.

She wrapped her arms across her breast but her back was cold as ice, and now she could feel the chill of the frost on her ankles.

The room was becoming darker and darker. Now it was impossible to see anything.

'I ought to . . . walk about,' Natalia told herself again and knew she was afraid.

Afraid of being alone, afraid perhaps although she knew it was nonsense, of the ghost which it was said haunted the old Mill.

It was very quiet. The rooks which had been 'cawing' in the distance as they went home to roost were now silent. Somewhere there was a drip of water, and occasionally a sudden scuffle as if a rat ran across the floor.

Natalia felt herself shiver in horror at the very thought.

An owl hooted a long way off, so far that she could barely hear it.

Then suddenly, unexpectedly, as she sat shivering and afraid, she heard footsteps! Heavy footsteps coming up the rickety stairway!

She wanted to cry out in gladness that someone had found her—that she was saved!

But as the cry came to her lips, she bit it back.

Perhaps it was not Lord Colwall . . . but a labourer bringing her some food.

She heard the bolt being pulled back and as the door swung open there was the golden light from a candle-lantern.

For a moment she could not see who held it, until as she stared, trying to penetrate the darkness behind the light, a mocking voice said a little thickly:

"Good evening, Your Ladyship . . ."

Chapter Eight

Captain Swing came into the room and held the lantern high above his head.

Natalia thought that he was looking at her in rather a strange manner, and instinctively she took a step backwards and put her hand up to the collar of her jacket.

He gave a low laugh and pulled the door to behind him. Then looking around, he saw a large wooden nail protruding from a wall on which he hung the lantern by its ring.

"Have you heard from His Lordship?"

Even to her own ears Natalia's voice sounded rather frightened.

"Not a word!" Captain Swing answered. "So I thought, My Lady, we might pass the time while we are waiting for his surrender by getting to know each other."

There was something in the tone of his voice and the way in which he slurred his words which told Natalia that the Captain not only had been drinking but was dangerous.

His eyes flickered over her and she felt a sudden apprehension—a fear that she had never known before in the whole of her sheltered life.

With a tremendous effort she raised her chin proudly.

"I have nothing to discuss with you, Captain Swing, as you must well know. If His Lordship has not answered your threatening letter, then doubtless he has

143

sent for the Military. Until they come to release me, I prefer to be alone."

"Brave words, My Lady!" Captain Swing said sneeringly. "But since your husband is treating me in such an arbitrary manner, it is up to you to make amends for his incivility."

He advanced across the floor as he spoke, and Natalia moved backwards until she was against the wall.

"I do not . . . know what you . . . mean," she faltered.

"I think you do," Captain Swing replied. "You are very pretty, and pretty women must learn to be generous with their favours."

By this time he was close beside her and put out his hand.

"Do not dare to . . . touch me!" Natalia cried.

Now that he had made his intentions plain, she managed to twist aside and rush to the other side of the small room.

The Captain had drunk too much to move swiftly, but there was no doubt that the liquor had inflamed him. His eyes in the light from the lantern were terrifying, as with a smile on his thick lips he pursued Natalia.

Again and again she avoided him, but she knew that because the room was small, she had little chance of escape.

Finally he pinioned her in a corner and laughed at her efforts as she twisted and fought against him.

"Let me go! Let me go!"

He was breathing heavily and she realised that his pursuit of her had excited him.

She made one tremendous effort to push him to one side, and then as they struggled he tripped her and she fell backwards on to the floor so violently that her head hit the bare boards.

For a moment it knocked her half-unconscious. Captain Swing flung himself upon her.

She felt nauseated by the brute force and the smell of him.

His breath exuded raw spirits, and his body pinioned hers as effectively as if she had been chained to the ground.

She wanted to scream, but she was breathless from fright and from her efforts to escape him.

Terrified she thought he would kiss her, and turned her face away, but instead he tugged violently at the front of her riding-jacket.

She put up her hands to prevent him—striking at him, trying to pull at his wrists.

But the buttons burst and now her jacket was open. He snatched the green scarf from her neck and flung it onto the floor.

The blouse she wore for riding was made of silk and tore easily beneath his fingers.

He was like an animal, plucking at the chemise next to her skin until her breasts were naked. It was then that Natalia screamed.

She screamed and screamed as his hands touched her and screamed again as he started pulling violently at her velvet riding-skirt.

It was tough and the waist-band resisted him, but brutal and primitive in his desires he had the strength of a wild beast.

Natalia was helpless beneath him.

She heard her own voice screaming and the sound of it echoing round the small room. Then she knew despairingly that her strength was failing and her efforts to fight off the maniac on top of her was of no avail.

She thought she must die of the horror of it. She thought she must go mad at the thought of what he was about to do.

"Help . . . me . . . God . . . help . . . me."

Suddenly there was a violent explosion which seemed to shake the whole building.

It was deafening in Natalia's ears, and Captain Swing collapsed on top of her, crushing her beneath his weight.

For a moment . . . everything seemed to go black . . .

Someone was pulling the Captain roughly from her body and she knew who it was!

She wanted to speak but her voice had died in her throat. She could only watch Lord Colwall—her eyes wide and terrified—as he dragged Captain Swing's body across the room by the collar of his coat.

For a moment Natalia was unable even to move her hands.

She felt paralized from the rough impact when Captain Swing had fallen on top of her, and the fear which seemed to have numbed her mind.

Then as she heard Lord Colwall going down the rickety stairs dragging the body with him, she put her hands slowly and feebly, as if they hardly belonged to her, across her naked breasts.

It was difficult to breathe, difficult to think, and yet she found herself listening and waiting for Lord Colwall to return.

She heard a splash in the Mill pool and then he was coming up the stairs again.

With an almost superhuman effort, Natalia tried to raise herself from the ground. He reached her while she was still making the attempt.

"Come," he said. "I will take you home."

She was trembling and so weak that even when he had drawn her to her feet he had to support her.

He picked up her scarf and put it round her neck. Then taking from his shoulders the black cloak he was wearing, he covered her with it and fastened the buckle.

She stood quite still, her hands across her breasts, her eyes wide with shock.

"It is all over, Natalia, you are safe," Lord Colwall said gently.

She walked unsteadily towards the door, his hand supporting her arm. As he left the room he lifted the lantern from the nail, and it lit their steps down the stair-way.

As she reached the bottom something large and warm hurled itself against her, raising his great head to lick her cheek.

It was Herald!

"You must thank Herald for finding you," Lord Col-wall said. "I felt certain that if anyone could track you down it would be he."

With his arm around Natalia he drew her outside the barn and she saw by the light of the half-moon climbing up the sky that there were two horses tied to a broken fence.

She knew one of the horses had belonged to Captain Swing, and that once he had reached the barn it would not have been difficult for Lord Colwall to guess where she was imprisoned.

His Lordship's horse was fidgeting a little, but the Captain's was quiet and apathetic.

Lord Colwall glanced at it.

"Wait one moment," he said.

He propped Natalia as if she was a doll against the doorway of the Barn. She watched him without speaking as he went to Captain Swing's horse, undid the girths and lifted the saddle from the animal's back.

Then he slipped off the bridle and walking the short distance to the Mill pool threw them in. There was a loud splash as they hit the water and Lord Colwall chucked the lantern after them.

He retraced his steps, saw that Captain Swing's horse was unconcernedly cropping the grass, and pick-ing Natalia up in his arms, he set her on the back of his stallion.

Just for a moment she balanced precariously, and then with the quickness of a man who is extremely athletic, Lord Colwall swung himself into the saddle behind her.

He put his left arm round her holding her close and picked up the reins.

Natalia turned her head to hide it against his shoul-der and then, as if the closeness of him released the tension that had gripped her, she burst into tears.

She cried despairingly, tempestuously, her whole body shaken by the violence of her reaction as a child will cry who has been frightened beyond en-durance.

"It is all right," Lord Colwall said soothingly, "You are safe."

His horse was moving slowly.

"You must forgive me," he went on, "if I was a long time in coming for you, but I returned home only just before dinner to find the note telling me you had been taken as a hostage."

His arm tightened around her and, although Natalia was still crying, she was listening.

"I had to make a quick decision," he continued, "whether to send for the Military, which would have taken a long time, to summon the farm labourers and force them—at pistol point if necessary—into telling me where that fiend had put you, or to try to find you myself!"

He paused for a moment as if remembering how hard the decision had been. Then he continued:

"I decided the best and quickest way would be to take Herald to the threshing barn where I guessed you had encountered the rioters."

Natalia was still crying. The tears were running down her cheeks and there was nothing she could do to stop them.

At the same time she was listening to Lord Colwall's deep voice, knowing that nothing mattered now he had found her and she was safe.

Even so, the evil from which she had so narrowly escaped still seemed to encompass her with a band of terror she could not break.

One of her hands clutched at the lapel of Lord Colwall's coat.

She wanted to be sure he was really there; she wanted to hold on to him; to know that she need not be stricken with that frantic, petrifying fear which had made her scream and scream as Captain Swing had lain on top of her.

"How could you have been so foolish," she heard Lord Colwall say, "as to ride alone without a groom?"

She did not reply and he answered his own question.

"They told me at the Castle you were coming to join

me, and how should you know there was danger for you, of all people, in this quiet countryside?"

There was a note of fury behind his words, and as if the very word "danger" evoked again the agony through which she had passed, Natalia went on crying.

Yet at the same time she knew within herself that gradually the comfort of Lord Colwall's presence, the feel of his arms encircling her, was dispersing much of the nightmarish terror which had overshadowed her.

'I am safe with His Lordship,' she told herself, 'and he is holding me close to him as I have always wanted him to do!'

She tried to feel the rapture that she had always known she would feel if she was ever in his arms.

Yet while her mind told her it was what she had craved, her body still under the spell of Captain Swing's violence, she could only shiver at the memory of the experience.

Natalia had never known violence and had never seen it.

Now she thought she would never be able to forget the weight of his body on top of hers, the roughness of his hands, or the lust in his eyes which had contorted his face until he had seemed like the very devil incarnate.

Moreover it had been an abject humiliation to realise how helpless she was, to learn that against brute strength a woman was completely and hopelessly impotent.

"Herald picked up your trail almost as soon as we left the barn," Lord Colwall was saying. "I could not imagine why he should be leading me through the willows by the bank of the stream. Then when we came to the old Mill and I saw that swine's horse waiting outside it, I knew I had been right to come alone."

His arm tightened around her as he said:

"I killed that man, Natalia. Do you hear me?"

Natalia did not answer, but he knew by the manner in which she hid her face even closer against his shoulder that she was listening to him.

"I killed him," Lord Colwall repeated, "and I am not ashamed of it! It was not murder. It was simply the destruction of a rat who deserved to die."

His voice was sharp with contempt. Then he continued:

"Because to make an explanation to the Magistrates must involve you, and because I do not wish anyone to know that you have been in contact with a man of his depravity and reputation, we will, neither of us, speak of this again."

He paused then said insistently:

"Swing is dead. He is finished. The last trace of him is lost in the depths of the Mill pool and the world will be a better place."

By now they were approaching the Castle. Lord Colwall looked up at the lights in the windows and the great stone building rising above the skeleton branches of the trees before he said urgently:

"Forget what has happend, Natalia. Forget that he so grossly insulted you. In future I will protect you better. No-one, I repeat, no-one must learn that you have suffered in this manner.'

There was so much solemnity in his tone that Natalia stopped crying.

She knew that they had reached the court-yard outside the front door because she could hear the sound of the gravel beneath the horse's hoofs.

"Leave all explanations to me," Lord Colwall commanded.

He drew the stallion to a standstill and now raising her head Natalia saw the golden light from the open doorway, and the Butler and a number of footmen waiting for them.

They would have' assisted her to alight from the saddle, but Lord Colwall jumped to the ground and lifted her down himself.

Natalia dropped her head and folded the cloak tightly round her.

"You have brought back Her Ladyship!" she heard the Butler exclaim.

"I found Her Ladyship imprisoned in the old Mill,"

Lord Colwall replied. "She is very cold and it was an unpleasant place for her to be alone in at night. Send food and wine up to her room immediately."

"Yes, M'Lord—of course, M'Lord."

The servants hurried to obey Lord Colwall's orders, and with his arm around Natalia he helped her slowly up the stairs.

Ellen was waiting on the landing outside her bedroom.

"Get Her Ladyship to bed," Lord Colwall said. "She is cold and hungry."

"Oh, M'Lady, we have been so worried about you!" Ellen exclaimed.

She led Natalia into the bed-room.

Lord Colwall turned and went downstairs again.

Ellen helped Natalia off with her cloak and gave an exclamation when she saw the buttons were burst from her jacket and her riding-blouse was torn.

"I . . . struggled with the . . . men who were . . . shutting me up," Natalia said as explanation.

She felt that Lord Colwall must have forgotten the condition of her clothes and that Ellen would be curious.

"I've never heard of such a thing, M'Lady!" Ellen ejaculated angrily.

"Do not speak of it to . . . the others," Natalia begged. "His Lordship would not like it known that anyone has been . . . rough with me."

"No, of course not, M'Lady," Ellen agreed.

Natalia's voice was very low and hoarse and she knew it was the shock of Captain Swing's attempt to ravish her which still made it difficult for her to speak.

She realised she had not said a word to Lord Colwall as he brought her home. She wished now she had been able to thank him.

'He saved me!' she said to herself, 'just as . . . my Knight would have . . . done.'

Lord Colwall, returning to the Castle the following day just after noon, thought with satisfaction of what he had to relate to Natalia.

It was a cold day but fine, and Lord Colwall riding his big black stallion looked strikingly handsome as he entered the court-yard and glanced up at the great grey stone building that was part of his heritage.

He had intended to see Natalia the previous evening before she went to sleep.

He had in fact gone upstairs after his own lonely dinner in the great Dining-Room and had knocked on her bed-room door. Ellen opened it and slipped outside to speak to him.

"Her Ladyship is sleeping, M'Lord."

"Did she have something to eat?"

"Yes, M'Lord, and a little of the wine to drink."

"I think Her Ladyship's clothes were in a rather unusual state—" Lord Colwall began.

"Her Ladyship told me, M'Lord, that the men who imprisoned her treated her somewhat roughly. She asked me not to speak of it, feeling Your Lordship would not wish it known amongst the other staff."

"No, and I am sure I can trust you, Ellen."

"I would do anything for Her Ladyship, M'Lord, and that's the truth!"

"I am glad to hear that," Lord Colwall said. "Do you think you should sit up with her?"

"I did suggest it, M'Lord, but Her Ladyship said it would disturb her to have someone in the room. She is sleeping quite peacefully at the moment and is very glad to be home."

"That is all I wanted to know," Lord Colwall said. "There is of course a bell which Her Ladyship can pull if she needs you."

"It rings in my bed-room, M'Lord, and I could be with Her Ladyship within a few seconds of her wanting me."

"Have you made up the fire?"

"Yes, M'Lord."

Ellen looked at Lord Colwall wonderingly.

It was very unlike His Lordship to be so solicitous, and yet, she told herself, he had always been one for planning things down to the smallest detail.

"I think I have thought of everything, M'Lord, and as I said, Her Ladyship has only to pull the bell and I will be with her before it even stops ringing."

"Thank you, Ellen."

Lord Colwall went downstairs again and Ellen, watching him go, thought how handsome he was and how proudly he carried himself.

'If only they could be really happy,' she sighed.

And then something told her there had been a new kindness and consideration in Lord Colwall's voice.

She wondered as she went to her own part of the Castle what had occurred the night before to make her Lady seem so distressed that morning.

She had served Natalia long enough to know when she was unhappy, and it had been impossible for her mistress to disguise the misery in her eyes or the droop of her lips.

Then as she watched Lord Colwall across the Park, it had seemed to Ellen as if her mood had changed completely. She had been eager and excited at the thought of hurrying after him.

'She deserves happiness,' Ellen said to herself. 'And so does he—after all he has been through!'

Before he left the Castle after breakfast Lord Colwall had enquired if Natalia had enjoyed a good night. The Butler had gone in search of Ellen and returned to say:

"Ellen has asked me to inform Your Lordship that, not having been summoned by Her Ladyship at the usual hour, she peeped into her bed-room a short while ago, and Her Ladyship was still asleep."

"Then do not awaken her," Lord Colwall had commanded. "The longer Her Ladyship sleeps, the better."

"Yes indeed, M'Lord. There's nothing like it," the Butler agreed. "and I'll give Ellen Your Lordship's instructions."

Now on his return at mid-day Lord Colwall hoped that Natalia would be awake; for he had much to tell her.

A groom was waiting at the front door to take his

horse. He swung himself from the saddle, patted the stallion on its shining black neck and walked up the steps.

He handed his hat to the Butler.

"Has Her Ladyship come downstairs yet?"

"No, M'Lord, but Ellen asked if Your Lordship would step upstairs for a moment."

Lord Colwall looked at the servant in surprise. He seemed about to say something and then changed his mind. Instead he turned towards the stair-case and walked up it slowly.

Ellen was waiting for him on the landing.

She curtsied and said:

"Will you come into Her Ladyship's bed-room, M'Lord?"

She opened the door and Lord Colwall preceded her into the room.

He looked at the bed as if he expected to see Natalia lying against the lace-edged pillow under the great four-poster. But it was empty!

He turned sharply with a look of enquiry in his eyes towards Ellen.

"Where is Her Ladyship?"

"That is what I don't know, M'Lord."

"What do you mean, you do not know?"

"She is not here, M'Lord."

Lord Colwall stared at her as if she had taken leave of her senses.

"What are you trying to say to me?" he asked.

"It's like this, M'Lord," Ellen said in a nervous voice. "I received your orders to let Her Ladyship sleep on. I didn't go into her room until about twenty minutes ago."

She glanced at Lord Colwall as if she feared she had done wrong.

"I thought Her Ladyship might be needing me and perhaps something had prevented the bell from ringing," she said in explanation. "I opened the door very quietly thinking that, if Her Ladyship was still asleep, I could creep out again. Then I stood and waited to hear

her breathing. I could not hear her and so I pulled
back the curtains."

"She was not there?" Lord Colwall asked.

"No, M'Lord. The bed was ruffled in such a way
that it looked from the door as though there was someone in it, but Her Ladyship had disappeared."

"She must have gone downstairs."

"No, M'Lord, the footmen in the Hall would have
seen her."

"She must be somewhere in the Castle—in the Nursery perhaps?"

"No, M'Lord, no-one has seen her."

"I cannot understand it!"

"Neither could I, M'Lord, but I went to the wardrobe to see if any of Her Ladyship's gowns were missing."

"And were any?"

"Look at this, M'Lord."

Ellen crossed the bed-room to the wardrobe which
stood on the far wall.

She pulled open the door and Lord Colwall saw the
rows and rows of beautiful and elaborate gowns that
had so entranced Natalia when she first arrived at the
Castle.

But Ellen did not concern herself with them.

Instead she pointed to something lying on the floor.

"Look at that, M'Lord!"

"What is it?" Lord Colwall asked in bewilderment.

He saw a heap of what appeared to be black ribbon
and bows of velvet.

"They come from a black gown belonging to Her
Ladyship," Ellen explained. "She had only one black
gown amongst those which came from London, and it
was a rather elaborate one. Almost too elaborate, I
thought, for a funeral or if Her Ladyship was forced
to wear mourning."

She paused and then as Lord Colwall made no com-
ment went on:

"Her Ladyship has taken off all the trimmings.
There they are, M'Lord, for you to see—the taffeta

frills, the velvet bows. She must have cut them away leaving the gown very plain without them."

"Why ever should she do that?" Lord Colwall demanded.

"I cannot understand it, M'Lord. There is something else, too."

Ellen opened another door, and now, following the direction of her finger, Lord Colwall saw that lying on the floor was a heap of white fur.

He looked at Ellen for explanation.

"It's the ermine lining, M'Lord, of Her Ladyship's travelling cape."

"Her travelling cape!" Lord Colwall exclaimed.

"Yes, M'Lord. There's nothing else gone as far as I can ascertain, except for a few of Her Ldayship's intimate garments. Just enough, I should say, to fill a small bag that one could carry in one's hand."

"And is there a bag missing?" Lord Colwall asked.

"Yes, M'Lord. The smallest baggage was kept in a cupboard next door to this room. The trunks were taken upstairs."

"And one is missing?"

"T'was only a small bag, M'Lord, rather a rough one, not as smart as the others, but it was useful for last-minute objects when we were travelling."

Lord Colwall walked across the room.

"You think, Ellen, that Her Ladyship has left the Castle?"

"She must have, M'Lord. There is no sign of her."

"Have you spoken of this to anyone?"

"No, M'Lord. I merely asked the footmen if they had seen Her Ladyship come downstairs. They replied they had been on duty since early this morning, and there has been no-one about except Your Lordship."

"You did not tell them why you asked?"

"No, M'Lord."

"Then if Her Ladyship left the Castle, she could not have gone by way of the front door."

"No, M'Lord. It'd be easy though to get out any other way. There are half a dozen doors into the garden, and three or four in the kitchen quarters."

"Her Ladyship must have walked," Lord Colwall remarked as if he spoke to himself. "If she had ordered a carriage from the stable it would have come to the front door."

"Of course, M'Lord."

"I cannot understand it!" Lord Colwall exclaimed. "And where could she have gone?"

There was a knock at the door.

"See who it is," Lord Colwall said sharply, "and do not let anyone come in."

"Very good, M'Lord."

Ellen went to the door and passed through it, partly closing it behind her.

Lord Colwall could hear her voice speaking and one of the footmen answering her. Then she returned and there was a letter in her hand.

"It appears, M'Lord," she said, "that there was a note addressed to you, downstairs by the entrance to the Dairy. The boot-boy found it earlier this morning, but he thought it was only a bill left by one of the tradesmen."

Ellen saw the frown on Lord Colwall's face.

"He did not take it to the pantry until a few minutes ago," she went on, "and now, in case it may be urgent, it has been brought upstairs."

She handed the letter to Lord Colwall as she spoke, and he took it from her with an expression in his eyes which she could not fathom.

It would be difficult for anyone, he thought, except for some nit-witted scullery boy, not to realise that the envelope was of the thick, expensive vellum used only by himself and Natalia.

He sat looking at the note as if he was afraid to open it.

Ellen moved tactfully away to another part of the room, ostensibly to pat up a cushion and put straight an ornament on a side-table that needed no adjustment.

Lord Colwall walked across to the window.

He knew the note was from Natalia and he longed to know its contents, yet at the same time he was afraid.

Why should she have gone away? Why should she have left the Castle?

He thought last night that he had re-assured her and that after she had cried so bitterly against his shoulder the horror of what she had passed through had been expunged.

Now he could not understand why she had disappeared without any warning. If she had wished to return to her parents, surely she would have told him so?

Besides, why should she go on foot? Stage-Coaches stopped in the village once or twice a day, but why would Natalia, with a stable full of every type of carriage at her command, wish to travel by Stage-Coach?

She had been unpredictable, he thought, as he turned the envelope over in his hand, ever since he had married her. He had not realised that he could find any woman so incomprehensible.

He had imagined it would be so easy to manage a young girl, and yet Natalia had defied and confounded him from the first moment of their marriage.

He thought of how he had raged at her the night before last in the Library.

He could see now the startled surprise in her large eyes, the sudden tremble of her lips, and he had known even as the words poured from his lips that she had not understood the reason for his fury.

She had looked so lovely sitting there with her arms around Herald.

She had looked somehow unsubstantial, and yet, as he well knew, she had a will almost equal to his own and a determination that he had been unable to break.

Everything had gone wrong!

His plans had mis-fired. The scheme which he had devised more than three years ago had been completely disrupted by one unsophisticated and inexperienced girl.

And now he knew that she had left him and he was afraid to learn the reason.

It was somehow incredible that he, so decisive, so autocratic, so unbending, should stand with her note in his hand, unable to bring himself to open it and read what it contained!

He was aware that Ellen was waiting and her curiosity was understandable.

Yet he knew it was not curiosity that he himself felt, but an apprehension that was almost like the anticipation of a physical blow.

Slowly, very slowly, he slit open the envelope and drew out its contents.

He had never seen Natalia's hand-writing before, but he thought he would have known it was hers even if it had lain amongst a hundred others!

There was something beautiful in the way she wrote; in the way she formed her letters. There was an imagination in the curves of the S's, the tails of the G's and the Y's, as well as something upright and a little proud in the T's and the L's.

Because he was looking at her hand-writing, for a moment Lord Colwall found it impossible to understand what Natalia had written.

There just seemed lines and lines of words that had no meaning, until with an effort he forced himself to read:

"My Lord, I know now I was wrong not to obey Your wishes and become, as You begged of me, Your Wife. I was so foolish that I did not realise until yesterday that my Love would have been enough for us both. Later you might have grown a little fond of Me, but I think I would have been content if I could make You happy.

But now it is too late: when I overheard what Your Lordship said to Sir James, You stressed that your Wife must be "pure and untouched". I could not stay, loving You as I do, and know that You looked at me with disgust because I can no longer fulfil the second of these Conditions. So, My Lord, I am going away.

I shall not go home and You will not be able to find me. Also I think that where I am going I shall not live very long. Then You will be free again to find Someone who will not fail You as I have done, and who, I pray, will give you happiness and a Son.

Please forgive me, My Lord, for all my faults and
failings and thank You for saving me last night. I love
You, as I have always loved You, so please sometimes
think kindly of Your most reprehensible but penitent
Natalia."

Lord Colwall read the note through and then, as if
the sense of it could not penetrate his mind, he read
it again.

Holding the letter in his hand he moved nearer to the
window to stare sightlessly out over the great expanse
of garden and Park.

He stood there so long without speaking that Ellen,
embarrassed, moved towards the door thinking she
should leave him alone.

As she reached it, Lord Colwall said in a voice she
hardly recognised:

"Her Ladyship has gone away for a short visit—
but she will return. You can be certain of that!"

"Yes, M'Lord. Thank you, M'Lord."

Ellen curtsied.

She looked at him, his head and shoulders silhouetted against the brightness of the sky. There was
something very strange about the look of him.

She had the remarkable feeling that he was a man
bewildered and lost in an unfamiliar world.

Then she told herself she was imagining things and
she left the room closing the door softly behind her.

Lord Colwall was alone.

Chapter Nine

Nanny was sitting by the Nursery fire. She was not crocheting nor was she sleeping.

She was waiting.

Every evening for the last week she had sat late after the rest of the household had gone to bed, expecting Lord Colwall to visit her. Now at last she heard his footsteps coming along the passage.

She looked into the fire, her face compassionate, her eyes wise with the knowledge of grown-up people who still remain children in their hearts.

Lord Colwall opened the Nursery door and crossed the room without speaking to seat himself in the armchair on the other side of the hearth.

Nanny made no attempt to rise; she merely looked at him and waited.

After a moment he said:

"Where can Her Ladyship be? I went as far as the Orphanage in Groucester today, but there was no sign of her there."

Nanny did not reply and after a moment he went on:

"I have visited every Orphanage in every adjacent town. I was so certain that she would go somewhere where there were children."

"I also should have expected that, M'Lord," Nanny murmured almost beneath her breath.

She realised that Lord Colwall had grown thinner in the last ten days.

He had lost, too, his aloof pride which had made him

seem as if he stood apart from everyone with whom he came in contact.

'He now looks human,' Nanny told herself.

It was a fact that His Lordship's coldness and impenetrable reserve had been exchanged for an air of urgency, and his expression of habitual cynicism had vanished.

"Did you realise how unhappy Her Ladyship was?" Lord Colwall asked suddenly.

"I knew that she loved you," Nanny answered quietly.

"How could I ever have imagined," Lord Colwall asked almost savagely, "that a girl who had seen me once, when she was a child, had been in love with me for three years?"

Nanny smiled.

"It was not only your handsome face, Master Ranulf! It was because Her Ladyship is not an ordinary young woman. She's sensitive, romantic, imaginative, and I'm as sure as I'm sitting here that if she'd not loved you, she would not have consented to marry you."

"You are right! Of course you are right!" Lord Colwall said. "But I did not understand."

"And now you do—?" Nanny asked quietly.

"I have to find her—I will find her!" he said harshly.

"When that little boy Timothy was here," Nanny said, "I used to listen to Her Ladyship telling him stories. The one he liked best and the one Her Ladyship always seemed to want to tell him, was about a Knight."

She saw the expression in Lord Colwall's eyes and continued:

"There was something in the way Her Ladyship spoke of this Knight which told me he meant a great deal to her. She must have dreamt about him as girls do about someone they love."

Lord Colwall turned his head to stare into the fire, but Nanny knew he was attentive to every word she said.

"Her Ladyship used to describe to Timothy," she went on, "the dangerous situations in which the Princess found herself, but always she was rescued just in the nick of time by her Knight."

There was a pause and then Nanny said quietly:

"I've a feeling, Master Ranulf, that you have to rescue her in the same way. It's a test, so to speak. I don't know whether I am making myself clear?"

"You are making yourself very clear, Nanny, and you are making complete sense. I should be able to find her just as I found her, or rather Herald did, the other night when she was imprisoned in the old Mill."

"If you found her then, Master Ranulf, you can find her now. Did she ever say anything which might give you a clue as to where she was likely to go?"

"Something she said?" Lord Colwall replied. "I did not think of that. I was only so convinced in my own mind that because the little orphan-boy meant so much to her, she would go to him, or to another like him."

"There are children in other places besides Orphanages," Nanny said.

"Yes, of course there are," Lord Colwall agreed. "but how can I start looking for the sort of place that Her Ladyship would have heard about? And why should she have said that I would not be able to find her and that she thought that where she was going, she would not live very long?"

"Her Ladyship said that?" Nanny exclaimed incredulously.

"Yes, she wrote that in the note she left for me," Lord Colwall answered.

"It must be a place then, that she had heard about," Nanny murmured.

"Or she has read about!" Lord Colwall ejaculated suddenly.

There was a light in his eyes that had not been there before. He rose quickly to his feet and pulled at the bell which hung beside the chimney-piece.

"I remember, Nanny," he said, "that when I came down to dinner the night before Her Ladyship left, she was reading the newspaper as I entered the Salon. I asked her if there was anything of interest in it, and after a moment she spoke to me of further riots of the farm labourers and the measures to be taken against them."

"That need not have been all that she read," Nanny remarked.

"No, of course not," Lord Colwall agreed.

There was silence and Nanny knew he was deep in thought.

Again she appreciated the fact that the expression on his face had changed a great deal since Natalia had gone away. His jaw-line was sharper and she knew by the dark lines under his eyes that he had not slept much.

There was no doubt that he was suffering, but the fact that his emotions stiffled for too long had now escaped his control improved rather than detracted from his looks.

'He has come alive again,' Nanny said to herself, 'and that's the truth.'

The door opened and a footman stood there who was obviously surprised at seeing His Lordship.

"You rang, M'Lord?"

"Bring me the newspapers for Wednesday, November tenth," Lord Colwall said.

"Very good, M'Lord."

The man had turned to obey him before Lord Colwall asked sharply:

"They will not have been destroyed?"

"Oh no, My Lord. The newspapers are always kept for a month in case Your Lordship should require a back-number."

"Then get them for me immediately."

The footman shut the door, Lord Colwall walked across the room to lay his hand on the piebald rocking-horse. He stroked its mane absent-mindedly.

And then he said in a voice in which there was no mistaking the pain behind the words:

"How can she look after herself? She is so inexperienced, so innocent. She has no knowledge of the world, and Ellen tells me she took no money with her."

"No money?" Nanny ejaculated.

"Perhaps a pound or two. That is all."

"Then how will she manage, M'Lord?"

"Do you suppose I have not thought of that?" he asked.

His voice was hard as he continued:

"I have been torturing myself night after night, imagining her in some dangerous situation, being insulted or hurt, crying for help, and my not being there to rescue her?"

There was agony in Lord Colwall's tone now and almost instinctively, as if he were still the child she had nursed when he was a baby, Nanny's hand went out towards him.

He did not see her gesture as he was still standing looking at the rocking-horse.

"It is all—my fault!" he said in a low voice.

As if she realised she must save him from his own despondency, Nanny said almost briskly:

"You'll find her, Master Ranulf. I'm sure of it. You must just use your brain and think where she could have hidden herself. I can't believe that Her Ladyship would deliberately do anything dangerous or foolish. She's too much sense for that!"

"But she does not know the evil and the dangers that lie in wait for someone as lovely as she is," Lord Colwall said hoarsely.

"We can only pray that God and his angels will protect her," Nanny said.

"—or her Knight," Lord Colwall murmured beneath his breath.

The footman brought the newspapers and put them neatly folded on a table which stood in the centre of the Nursery.

Lord Colwall crossed the room eagerly towards them. He picked up *The Times*. Then he said:

"I am almost certain it was the *Morning Post* Her Ladyship was reading when I entered the Salon."

He took the newspaper in both hands.

"Yes, here is what she must have read about the

new penalties imposed by the Government on rioters."

He looked down the page and then he gave an exclamation.

"Nanny!" he said urgently, "listen to this!"

"ABNORMAL DEATH RATE IN WORKHOUSES"

"In answer to a question in the House of Commons the Home Secretary agreed that last year's deaths in Workhouses all over the country were considerably above normal. It was due, he explained, to a new fever as yet unidentified, which had resulted in a sudden increase in mortality among workhouse dwellers of all ages. Children had of course accounted for the majority of the deaths, although there was also a large increase of mortality amongst the aged. There was little that could be done about it, but the Charity Commissioners and Poor-Law Administrators were keeping close watch on their local Workhouses."

Lord Colwall finished reading the report aloud. Then he said with a sudden light in his eyes:

"I had forgotten that there are children in the Workhouses. Tomorrow morning I will start a systematic tour of every one that is within a range of thirty miles."

"Do that, Master Ranulf!" Nanny exclaimed.

"Shall I go first to Hereford?"

"I have a feeling," Nanny answered, "although I may be wrong, that if Her Ladyship is hiding from you, she would not hide in Hereford where you have so many meetings. Also she might easily be recognized by one of the friends who came to your wedding."

"No, of course not. That is sensible," Lord Colwall replied. "And the Stage-Coach could have taken her to Malvern, or Worcester or any of the towns the other side of the hills. I will start first thing in the morning."

He threw the newspaper down on the table.

Then he walked to the fire-side and did something he had not done for very many years. He bent down and kissed his old Nurse on the cheek.

"Thank you, Nanny," he said.

The Workhouse was an ugly, bare building, built of grey stone with barred windows. There was a court-yard in front of it and a high wall with heavy gates, spiked on top, which Lord Colwall knew would be locked at night.

They were open now to allow his curricle, drawn by two horses, to pass through.

The gate-keeper was a very old man with white hair, quivering hands and bloodshot eyes that were running with the cold from the wind.

It appeared to Lord Colwall that the man's clothing was far from adequate for the duties he carried out.

His Lordship drew his horses up outside the some-what forbidding entrance and handed the reins to the groom, who had jumped down from the small seat on the back of the curricle.

Without waiting, as he usually did, for his servant to knock at the door, Lord Colwall himself raised the knocker and rapped sharply.

At first he thought his request for attention had gone unnoticed. Then he heard slow, shuffling feet and the door was opened by another old man, so bent with age that his nose seemed to be half-way down his chest.

"I wish to speak with either the Mistress or the Master of this Workhouse," Lord Colwall said in a commanding tone.

The old man made a gesture which invited him in and he walked through the doorway into a paved pas-sage.

The place smelled strongly of unwashed bodies, old age and drains, which Lord Colwall found very dis-tasteful. The old man shuffled ahead of him and opened the door of a room.

It was obviously the private Sitting-Room of the Keepers of the Workhouse. It was furnished without taste, but there were faint touches of homeliness about it, including a fire burning brightly in a well-polished grate.

A door in the opposite wall opened and a woman came in. She was large, middle-aged and had an aggressive, authoritative manner which made Lord Colwall dislike her on sight.

She had however either been told that her visitor was important or she had seen his curricle outside, for there was an almost ingratiating smile on her thin lips as she said politely:

"Good day, Sir. What can I do for you? Are you a County Inspector, by any chance?"

"I am not," Lord Colwall answered. "I am making private enquiries as to whether you have recently employed or admitted a young woman to these premises."

He saw the look in the Mistress's eyes before she spoke, and ejaculated:

"You have!"

"I am not accepting, Sir, that you are right in your surmise concerning the presence here of the person you seek," the Mistress answered. "The inhabitants of this place come and go, and I assure you it is extremely difficult to find assistants."

"But you have found one," Lord Colwall said.

"I was left empty-handed when the last batch of children of over six years old were taken to the factories," the Mistress said, and her tone suggested that she thought Lord Colwall was finding fault. "Heaven knows, the little varmints weren't much help, but at least they could work better than those I've left."

"I am not suggesting that in seeking as assistant you were doing anything wrong," Lord Colwall said evenly. "I merely wish to know who she is? What is her name?

"I thought there was something strange about her," the Mistress remarked viciously, "the moment I saw her, and I says to myself: 'You're either in trouble, or a run-away apprentice.' And that's the truth, Sir, isn't it?"

"I wish to see this girl," Lord Colwall answered. "Is she small and fair?"

"You can see her, Sir, and welcome," the Mistress said. "I suppose as usual I shall be left to do everything for myself. How can one woman cope with what we have in now? Three loonies; fourteen old people all getting on for eighty; four tramps and ten children. Ten! I tell you, Sir, it's too many!"

"I wish to see your new assistant," Lord Colwall said, interrupting the flow of complaints which he felt might go on endlessly.

"She'll be up on the top floor with the children," the Mistress replied. "I can't get her away from them, though I have told her again and again that I need her help downstairs with the decrepit and senile."

As she spoke the woman led the way out into the passage and started to climb the narrow stairs which led to the top floor of the Workhouse.

Lord Colwall had a glimpse of a room bare of furniture except for a few chairs, with two spinning wheels standing unused in the corner. The occupants were huddled around the walls, some of them sitting on the floor.

"Is there no heating?" he asked sharply.

"Heating?"

The Mistress turned her head to look at him incredulously.

"Where do you think the money comes from for that sort of luxury? The Parish provides for only the bare necessities and that's too good for most of them as is in here."

She spoke almost venomously and continued to climb the stairs, holding up her skirts with both hands.

The top floor was little more than a garret. The gabled windows that opened on to the tiled roof had several panes of glass broken in each of them. One or two of the apertures had been stuffed with rags.

There was a row of beds, some of them tied up with string, and on each there was one thin, tattered blanket.

At the far end of the room all the children were clustered in a little circle, except for one child who was lying on a bed.

The children were chattering and did not hear the Mistress approach, sailing down the centre of the room like a ship in full sail with Lord Colwall behind her.

Then as he neared them he could see that they were standing around a slender figure who was kneeling on the floor beside a bucket. She was scrubbing.

"Gray!"

The Mistress's voice, harsh and ugly, seemed to echo round the garret.

"How many times must I tell you not to do the work which that lazy little Letty should do? I told her to scrub the floor after she made a mess of it, and scrub it she shall! Get her off that bed and give her the brush, or I'll beat her into doing what she's told."

Natalia straightened her back and looked up at the Mistress who was now towering over her.

"Letty is only four, Ma'am, and she is feeling ill."

"She'll soon be feeling a good deal iller if she doesn't do what I've ordered her to do!" the Mistress replied sharply. "And here, Gray, is someone to see you. I don't suppose you expected your past would catch up with you so quickly."

The woman spoke spitefully and now Natalia saw Lord Colwall.

Their eyes met and neither of them could move.

She was very pale, and it seemed to him that she had grown so thin that the skin was stretched taut over her bones.

Very quietly, almost as if he were afraid he might frighten her, Lord Colwall said:

"I have come to take you home, Natalia."

She rose to her feet and he saw that she was wearing a rough apron of sacking over her black dress; her fair hair was dragged back from her forehead and pinned into a bun at the nape of her neck.

She put the large scrubbing-brush she held in her right hand into the bucket of water and set the bucket against the wall. As she moved it, Lord Colwall saw that her hands were red and sore.

"There's no use putting that bucket aside," the Mistress said sharply. "Letty! Get off that bed and finish the floor and the rest of you children move out of the way, or it'll be the worse for you!"

Slowly Natalia took off her apron and hung it on

a nail. Then she turned to one of the beds and picked up her cloak which had obviously been used as an extra covering.

She put it round her shoulders and as she did so the children began to cry:

"Don't leave us, Miss! Don't go away! Ye said ye'd stay!"

Their voices, shrill and protesting, rang out as they surged around her, hanging on to her cloak and her hands, their faces turned up to hers, their bodies pitiably thin under the rags they wore for clothes.

"I have to go now," Natalia said gently, "but I will come back to see you, I promise you I will."

"Ye promise? Ye promise? Ye won't forget?"

"No, I can never forget!"

Natalia disentangled herself from their clinging hands without looking at Lord Colwall. He stood watching her, in his elegance incredibly out of place in the cold barren garret.

As if something was happening which she did not understand, the Mistress turned angrily on the children:

"Get on with your work, you lazy little varmints! You've no right to be standing about doing nothing. You're paupers. Work, or you don't eat! This place is called a Workhouse and that's what it has to be, or I'll know the reason why!"

Lord Colwall saw Natalia wince at the woman's roughness, and then with a little helpless gesture as if she knew she could do nothing about it, she pulled her hood over her head and walked down the room towards the stair-way.

She did not wait to hear what Lord Colwall said to the Mistress, but proceeded through the front door and saw the curricle waiting for her outside.

Blindly, almost as if she were walking in her sleep, she stepped into it, and by the time Lord Colwall had seated himself in the driving-seat and picked up the reins, the groom had covered her with a fur rug.

"You will not be too cold?" Lord Colwall asked, as

if they were setting out on an ordinary drive from the Castle. "I ought to have brought a closed carriage, but I knew that I could travel faster in the curricle."

"I am . . .all right," Natalia answered.

They were the first words she had spoken to him and he heard the tremor in her voice. He said nothing more, merely busying himself with driving as swiftly as horses could travel back around the hills to the Castle.

There was, he thought, nothing they could say to each other with the groom within hearing. In fact Lord Colwall knew that what was of primary importance was to get Natalia home.

He had been deeply shocked by the pallor of her face and her emaciation. She had grown so thin that it seemed as if she might float away in the mist and be lost to him forever.

It was with a sense of relief that he saw his home high above the trees, and soon they were climbing the long drive.

He drew up outside the front door and pulled the horses to a standstill.

The Butler ran down the steps to assist Natalia to alight.

"Welcome home, M'Lady."

"Thank . . . you," Natalia answered.

Her voice was very low, and now as she reached the hall she allowed her cloak to be taken from her, and almost automatically she walked towards the Salon.

A flunkey opened the door and she moved over the thick carpet towards the fire.

She had almost reached it when she heard the door close and turned to see Lord Colwall advancing towards her.

For a second he saw a sudden light in her eyes, and then as he drew nearer it faded and was replaced by an expression which he knew was one of fear.

She looked at him, made a little inarticulate sound and slipped down onto the floor at his feet.

He picked her up in his arms, and realising that

she was unconscious he carried her from the Salon, across the Hall and up the stairs.

As he passed the Butler, he said sharply:

"Send for Nurse."

But when he reached the landing outside Natalia's bed-room, he found Nanny was there waiting for him and beside her was Ellen.

"You've found Her Ladyship! You've found her!" Ellen exclaimed ecstatically.

Lord Colwall did not answer. He carried Natalia into the room and set her down on the big four-poster, laying her very gently against the lace-edged pillows.

She looked so white, so frail in her black dress, dingy and dirty and so different from the elegant creation it had once been.

"Is she all right, Nanny?" he asked and there was a note of desperate anxiety in his voice.

"I think she's fainted, Master Ranulf," Nanny answered. "Leave Her Ladyship to us. We'll get her into bed and, judging by the looks of her, she needs something to eat."

"I will go and speak to the Chef," Lord Colwall said, as if glad to be able to take some action.

"Nourishing broth," Nanny said, and busied herself with Natalia.

"No . . . please don't touch her! . . . She is so small . . . she does not . . . understand . . ."

Natalia's words were a cry. Then someone said gently:

"Wake up, Natalia, you are dreaming. Wake up, it is only a nightmare."

She opened her eyes and saw Lord Colwall's face not far from hers. She felt a sudden surge of happiness at the sight of him . . . before she remembered and her eyes darkened . . .

"For God's sake, my darling, do not be afraid of me!"

The words seemed to burst from him. Then he said quickly, speaking as if were ashamed of his lack of self-control:

"You are at home. You are safe, and nothing shall upset you, I promise you."

The fear in Natalia's eyes was replaced with surprise.

It seemed to him as if she held her breath.

"Nanny told me that when you awoke I was to give you some soup to drink. It is over here."

It was night-time, Natalia realised, as he moved away from the bed, There was only the light from the flames leaping high in the fire-place and of several candles to cast a warm glow around the bed and leave the corners of the room in shadow.

'It must be very late,' Natalia thought to herself.

She saw that Lord Colwall was wearing a robe of dark blue brocade, and she felt that had it been earlier, Nanny or Ellen would have been with her.

She must have slept for hours, and now she remembered vaguely that she had been awakened several times to be given something to drink, a soup that seemed to warm her body and make her feel alive again.

She had thought sometimes that she would never be anything but cold and hungry until she died.

Lord Colwall was busy at the table and she could see that he was pouring from a jug which stood on a silver tray heated by a candle-burner.

He carried the cup carefully across the room to her.

She raised herself higher on the pillows and he sat down on the bed facing her.

"I want you to drink every drop," he said as he handed her the cup, "and then I have something to tell you."

She looked at him enquiringly before obediently she raised the cup to her lips.

Her fair hair hung loosely over her shoulders and he saw that she was wearing one of the diaphanous nightgowns that had been part of her trousseau.

In the few short hours that she had been back at the Castle, sleeping with an exhaustion that was almost frightening, some of the tension and sharpness seemed to have gone from her small face.

She looked very young and very pathetic, Lord Colwall had thought, when Nanny had brought him into the room to see her asleep.

"She is all right, Nanny?" he had asked when the Nurse had come from the bed-room to find him waiting on the landing outside.

"Come and see for yourself, Master Ranulf."

Nanny had known without being told that Lord Colwall was apprehensive as he had followed her into the bed-room to stand looking down at Natalia, her eye-lashes dark against her pale cheeks, her hair halo-ing her thin face.

"I don't think her Ladyship's had a mite to eat since she left here," Nanny whispered. "She said it was impossible for her to swallow anything when the children were so hungry."

She saw Lord Colwall's jaw tighten as she went on:

"Heaven knows what sort of place she's been in, Master Ranulf, but there are bruises on her back which she says she received when trying to stop a child from being beaten."

Lord Colwall clenched his fingers together and his knuckles were white.

"It's my belief," Nanny said softly, "that Her Ladyship'll have no peace until something is done about those children."

She saw the expression on his face, then without a word he was gone from the room and she heard him running downstairs.

Now Natalia had finished her soup and handed the cup back to Lord Colwall.

"As you have been so good," Lord Colwall said, "I will tell you something which I know will please you."

She looked up at him expectantly.

"I sent two carriages this afternoon to collect all the children from the Workhouse and take them to our own Orphanage," he said. "I have promised Mrs. Moppam she shall have still further help, and I have sent practically all the food there was in the Castle to feed them in the meantime."

The light in Natalia's eyes seemed to transfigure her face.

"You did . . . that?" she breathed hardly above a whisper. "Thank you . . . Thank you."

She put out her hands as she spoke with a gesture eloquent of gratitude. Then as he took them in his, she saw how rough and red they were and would have taken them away, but he raised them to his lips.

She felt herself quiver at the touch of his mouth on her skin.

"You must rest," he said in a deep voice, "but first I have something more to tell you."

"What is . . . it?" Natalia asked.

"I have promised the men on this Estate ten shillings a week wages, with two shillings extra for every child and the same for any elderly dependent."

He felt Natalia's fingers tighten on his as he went on:

"They have agreed to work the threshing-machine, but they will receive two shillings each per day threshing money. Next year we will take one thousand acres more into cultivation, which will mean more work and more money for every man."

"Thank you . . . Oh, thank . . . you!"

There were tears on Natalia's cheeks but when her eyes met Lord Colwall's it was as if neither of them could look away.

With an obvious effort Lord Colwall said:

"You must go to sleep. I will leave the door open between our rooms so that if you cry out I shall hear you, but now there is no reason for any more nightmares."

He would have risen from the bed as he spoke, but Natalia held on to one of his hands.

"I do not . . . wish to be . . . alone," she said almost inaudibly.

"Then I will stay with you," Lord Colwall replied in his deep voice, "but oh, my dearest heart, get well quickly! There is so much more I want to tell you, so much more that we can do together, and you will never be alone again, if I can help it!"

"Do you . . . mean that?"

"You know I mean it," he answered. "Do you not realise by now, Natalia, that I love you? It has been an agony beyond words these past ten days when I thought I would never find you again."

"I thought you . . . would not . . . want me to . . . stay."

"How could you think such a thing?" he asked. "You know I want you. I have always wanted you, but I did not realise how much until that devil took you away as a hostage and I did not know where to find you. I knew when I brought you home in my arms that you meant everything to me."

"The night before . . ." Natalia faltered, "in the . . . Library, you . . . sounded as if you . . . hated me . . ."

"I was crazy!" Lord Colwall declared. "It was because I felt so frustrated at your refusal to be my wife. I was at the same time fighting against admitting to myself that I loved you."

He felt Natalia's fingers trembling in his and he said:

"I loved you really from the first moment I saw you, but I vowed to myself that I would never again suffer as I had suffered in the past. So I fought against the enchantment of you every inch of the way!"

He gave a little laugh.

"If I suffered in the past, I have forgotten now what it felt like. For these past days I have suffered all the agonies of hell wondering where you were, desperately afraid of what might have happened to you."

"I thought . . . you would soon . . . forget me."

"How could I do that?" Lord Colwall asked simply. "You have captured my whole heart. It no longer belongs to me, but to you."

"Is this . . . true?"

"It is true, my beloved, completely and absolutely true. I love you now and you must teach me to love you in the way you want to be loved."

He bent his head as he spoke and kissed her hands again.

"They are so red and . . . ugly," Natalia murmured.

"They are beautiful, my dearest, because they are

yours, just as everything about you is all the loveliness
I ever want of life."

He drew in a deep breath.

"I have realised these past days that I have been
prizing all the wrong things. I know now that my possessions, even the Castle itself, are of no importance
beside the fact that you love me! One day I hope to be
able to make you understand what you mean to me."

He looked at Natalia as he spoke and saw the tears
come into her eyes again.

"This has been too much for you," he said quickly.
"You must go to sleep now, my darling, and we will
talk about everything in the morning. I will not leave
you alone. I will sleep on the sofa, so if you want me,
I shall be here."

There was a moment's silence and then Natalia said
hesitatingly:

"You might be . . . cold, and that . . . would worry
me. Could you not . . . get into bed? . . . It is very . . .
big."

For a moment Lord Colwall was absolutely still,
until he said in a voice which strove to be normal:

"As you say—it is very big."

He rose and walked to the fire to put on more coal
and logs. Then he blew out the candles behind the
curtains beside Natalia and walked around to the other
side of the bed.

There was only one candle burning there, and he
extinguished it before taking off his robe, he slipped
between the sheets.

As Natalia had said, the bed was very large and
there was a wide space between them.

She lay against the pillows watching the flames leaping high over the new logs. She did not turn her face
towards Lord Colwall, but she knew he was lying on
his back, straight and still.

After a moment she said in a very small voice:

"There is . . . something I . . . want to ask . . . you."

"What is it?" he enquired.

She did not reply and as if he knew she was shy

and embarrassed, he turned towards her, resting on his elbow to raise himself so that he could look down at her face.

"What is it?" he asked again.

"Do I . . . now that I have been . . . touched," she whispered, "disgust . . . you?"

For a moment it seemed as if Lord Colwall struggled to find words with which to answer. Then he moved closer to her and putting out his hand he very, very gently pulled her nightgown off her shoulders.

She made no movement as he bent his head and kissed first one of her small rose-tipped breasts, then the other. He replaced the nightgown and said in a voice that was unsteady:

"When you will let me, I will kiss you all over your perfect body. That is the real answer to your question."

He drew in his breath.

"You must go to sleep, my precious, you have been through so much. I must not tire you."

He spoke as if he admonished himself rather than her.

"Will you . . . kiss me . . . goodnight?"

Lord Colwall hesitated and then slowly, holding himself in an iron control, bent forward.

His lips sought her cheek, but she moved so that it was her mouth he kissed. At first there was only the faint touch of their lips, until suddenly it seemed to Natalia as if the whole room was filled with a brilliant light.

She felt a sudden thrill run through her which was like a sword piercing every nerve in her body.

Then Lord Colwall's arms were round her and he was kissing her frantically, passionately, demandingly.

She had known this was what it would be like to be kissed with love. She knew an ecstasy, a rapture that was beyond anything she had ever imagined or had dreamt was possible.

She put her arms round his neck and as she did so he raised his head.

"I love you! God, how I love you!" he cried. "Be

kind to me Natalia, I did not know love was like this. But I would not frighten you, my darling. I must give you time."

She made a little sound that was half a laugh of unbridled happiness.

Then she drew his head closer until his lips once again were on hers.

She knew there was no need for time, or words, or explanations.

This was love!

This was what she always knew they should feel for each other.

This was the wonder and glory of being not two people but one, of being close and indivisible, part of a joy and rapture not of this world, but of the Divine force which pouring through them, made them as Gods.

ABOUT THE AUTHOR

BARBARA CARTLAND, the celebrated romantic author, historian, playwright, lecturer, political speaker and television personality, has now written over 150 books. Miss Cartland has had a number of historical books published and several biographical ones, including that of her brother, Major Ronald Cartland, who was the first Member of Parliament to be killed in the War. This book had a Foreword by Sir Winston Churchill.

In private life, Barbara Cartland, who is a Dame of the Order of St. John of Jerusalem, has fought for better conditions and salaries for Midwives and Nurses. As President of the Royal College of Midwives (Hertfordshire Branch), she has been invested with the first Badge of Office ever given in Great Britain, which was subscribed to by the Midwives themselves. She has also championed the cause for old people and founded the first Romany Gypsy Camp in the world.

Barbara Cartland is deeply interested in Vitamin Therapy and is President of the British National Association for Health.